ISLAND OF THIEVES

JOSH LACEY

Houghton Mifflin Harcourt
Boston New York

To Bella

Text copyright © 2011 by Josh Lacey

First published in Great Britain in 2011 by Andersen Press Limited.

All rights reserved. Originally published in hardcover in the United States by
Houghton Mifflin, an imprint of Houghton Mifflin Harcourt Publishing Company, 2012.

For information about permission to reproduce selections from this book,
write to Permissions, Houghton Mifflin Harcourt Publishing Company,
215 Park Avenue South, New York, New York 10003.

www.hmhbooks.com

The text of this book is set in Adobe Caslon Pro.

The Library of Congress has cataloged the hardcover edition as follows:
Lacey, Josh.
Island of Thieves / by Josh Lacey.
p. cm.
1. Drake, John, fl. 1577–1580—Juvenile Fiction. 2. Drake, Francis, Sir, 1540?–1596—Juvenile
fiction. [1. Drake, John fl. 1577–1580—Fiction. 2. Drake, Francis, Sir, 1540?–1596—Fiction.
3. Buried treasure—Fiction. 4. Uncles—Fiction. 5. Islands—Fiction. 6. Peru—Fiction.
7. Adventure and adventurers—Fiction. 8. Mystery and detective stories.] I. Title.
PZ7.L128Is 2012
[Fic]—dc23

ISBN: 978-0-547-76327-9 hardcover
ISBN: 978-0-544-10485-3 paperback

Manufactured in the United States of America
DOC 10 9 8 7 6 5 4 3 2 1

4500431909

1

I *didn't mean to burn down our garden shed.* But now I'm glad I did. If I hadn't, none of this would have happened. The island. The gold. It was all because of burning down that shed.

The first day of vacation I was sitting in there playing with a box of matches. Striking one. Watching it burn. Blowing it out. Throwing the dead stick on the floor and reaching for another.

I was bored.

You're not allowed to say that word in our house.

Only boring people get bored, says Dad. *Interesting people can always find something to be interested in.*

You can't be bored, says Mom. *There's so much to do here! Why don't you play a game? Or call a friend? Or go for a bike ride?*

But I didn't feel like doing any of that stuff. So I hid in the shed and played with matches.

Suddenly I smelled smoke. I looked around. Flames were blazing up the walls. One of the matches must have still been burning when I dropped it on the floor. I sprang at the door, wrenched it open, and threw myself outside.

As I rolled across the grass, my clothes smoking, I saw my mom standing at the French windows, her mouth open in a silent scream. Then she ran to get her phone.

By the time the fire engines arrived, the shed had burned itself out. They drenched it anyway, making sure no sparks blew into any of the neighbors' houses. The chief fireman gave me a long lecture about fire safety. So did Mom. And Dad. They were still discussing how to punish me when the phone rang. It was Mrs. Spencer, calling to say that she was very sorry, but they really couldn't have me to stay. What if I burned down *their* shed too? Or even their house?

"It was an accident," said Dad. "He'll never do anything like it again."

But Mrs. Spencer wouldn't listen.

Dad sat at the kitchen table with his head in his hands. "I don't believe it," he groaned. "We'll have to take him with us."

"We can't," said Mom.

"Then what are we going to do?"

"Someone will have him."

"Oh, yes?" asked Dad. "Who?"

My parents were having their first vacation together *without children* since my big sister, Grace, was born. My kid brother, Jack, was staying with his friend Bongo. Grace was staying with her friend Ruby. I would have been staying with Finn Spencer, but his parents wouldn't have me now. After the shed incident, neither would anyone else.

"I don't mind staying here," I told my parents.

"No chance," said Dad.

I had another suggestion. "I could share Gran's room at the Home. I like playing chess with her friend Isaac. And the food's not bad."

But Mom vetoed that, too. "If no one will have you, we'll just have to cancel the vacation."

That was when Dad panicked. He called everyone he knew.

Everyone he could think of.

Even his brother.

Which was how I came to be sitting in the back of the family wagon at half past five on that Tuesday morning, whizzing down the interstate toward New York City.

Apparently I'd met Uncle Harvey a few times at weddings and funerals, but he'd never been to visit us in Norwich and I couldn't even remember what he looked like. Just like Dad, he was British but lived in the States, although in his case I didn't know why. Dad came here because he met Mom and married her and she wanted to be near her own parents when Grace was born. Uncle Harvey wasn't married and had no kids. I guess he just preferred New York to London, which makes sense; it's cold and damp over there and the food's terrible.

The drive took hours. By the time we finally made it to

Uncle Harvey's street, Dad was flipping out. "We're going to miss the plane," he said, breathless with panic. "I knew we should have left earlier."

"We're going to be fine," said Mom calmly. "Look, we're here already. That's number nineteen."

Dad double parked, grabbed my bag from the trunk, and scanned the street for traffic cops, then raced up the steps and rang the bell. Mom and I followed right behind him. We stood on the top step, looking at the paint peeling off the front door and the trash bags stacked against a lamppost, spilling tin cans and orange peels. Two women jogged past. A man came out of another brownstone wearing a blue suit and carrying a racing bike. He put the bike in the road and swung himself onto the seat.

Dad rang the bell again. "Where the hell is he?"

"Simon!" said Mom.

"Sorry," said Dad. "But where is he?"

"Asleep," I mumbled. "If he has any sense."

"He can't be asleep. He knows we're coming." But Dad took out his phone and called Uncle Harvey. There was a long pause. Then: "Hello? Harvey? Where are you? We're outside! Didn't you hear the bell? It doesn't matter. Forget it. Could you let us in?"

Six minutes later (Dad timed it), the front door was opened by an unshaven man wearing a long silk bathrobe decorated with yellow butterflies. "Simon! Sarah! How lovely to see you!"

I could see the relief on my parents' faces. When Uncle

Harvey hadn't answered the door, they really thought they'd have to take me to Nassau. Their vacation would have been ruined. Now they could hand me over and get away for a whole week of sunbathing, reading books by the pool, and smoochy candlelit dinners.

"Here's Tom," said Mom, pushing me forward. "He's very excited about staying so near Greenwich Village. Aren't you?"

"Hi," I said.

Uncle Harvey said hi back and shook my hand. He was taller than my dad, and thinner, too, and he looked much younger, although I knew the actual age difference was only two years and five months.

Mom said, "Are you sure you don't mind doing this?"

"I'm looking forward to it," said Uncle Harvey. He had a mischievous smile. "We're going to have a wild time together."

"Not too wild," said Dad. "Tom's been in enough trouble recently."

"That sounds interesting. What type of trouble? What have you done?"

"Oh, nothing much," I said. "Everyone just likes to get annoyed with me all the time."

"I know *exactly* what you mean," said Uncle Harvey.

I knew he didn't. He was just saying so to be nice. But I still appreciated it.

Dad gave me a quick, awkward hug. "Bye, Tom. Be good."

"Bye, Dad. Have a great vacation."

Mom kissed me. Then she stepped back and looked at me nervously. "I hope we're doing the right thing. You *will* behave yourself, won't you?"

"Of course he will," said Uncle Harvey. "Now stop worrying. I hereby give you permission to enjoy yourselves. Get thee to the airport and have a glass of wine."

They didn't argue. Just rushed down the steps and ran along the street to their car, not wanting to give my uncle the chance to change his mind.

We stood on the step together, Uncle Harvey and I, watching Mom and Dad drive off. Then my uncle turned to me and said, "So, Tom. Here we are."

"Yup," I said. "We're here."

"It's nice to see you after all these years."

"Uh, you too."

"You look exactly how your father looked when he was your age. Maybe you look like me, too. What do you think?" He turned his head from side to side, showing me his profile.

I stared at my uncle's face, searching for some connection between him and my father and myself, and finally I said, "I think we might have the same nose."

"Of course we do," said Uncle Harvey. "It's the Trelawney nose. Passed from generation unto generation. Without this nose, you can't be a Trelawney. Now let's go inside."

His apartment was on the fourth floor. As we trudged up the stairs together, Uncle Harvey said, "There is one thing

I have to warn you about. I didn't want to tell your father. I thought he might be upset. But you're not going to mind, are you?"

"Depends what it is," I said.

"Give me a chance and I'll tell you. When your father rang, I said you could stay in my flat, and you can. The only thing is, I won't actually be here. I've got to go abroad. On urgent business. But you can look after yourself, can't you?"

"No problem," I said.

"Are you sure?"

"Oh, yeah. I'll be fine."

"You'll have a wonderful time." He opened the door of his apartment and led me inside. "This is the perfect place for a bachelor. Treat it as your own. Invite friends round. Have parties. It's all yours. Does that sound OK?"

"That sounds great," I said.

"Good. I did try and explain this to your father, but he got so cross with me, I had to say I'd change my plans."

"He's been looking forward to this vacation for fifteen years," I explained. "He and Mom haven't been away together without kids since Grace was born. Not even for a weekend."

"That's what he said. I didn't think he'd be very happy about you staying here alone—"

"He wouldn't."

"—so I thought we needn't tell him. Is that terrible?"

"No," I said. "That's fine."

"You really don't mind?"

JOSH LACEY

"When you gotta go, you gotta go."

"I'm glad you see it like that, Tom. Strictly speaking, you're probably a bit young to be left alone, aren't you?"

"I'll be fine," I said, already imagining how I would spend a week alone in New York City. And then, not wanting to discuss whether it was actually legal to leave me by myself in an apartment for a week, I asked, "Where are you going?"

"Peru," said my uncle.

"Wow. Cool. What are you doing there?"

"Oh, it's a long story."

"I've got time."

"It's also a secret."

"I won't tell anyone — I promise."

Uncle Harvey shook his head. "I'm sorry, Tom. You might be my nephew, but I hardly know you. How could I possibly trust you with such an important secret?"

"We could do a deal," I said.

"A deal? What kind of deal?"

8

2

I've actually just come back from Peru," said Uncle Harvey. We were sitting at his kitchen table, drinking grapefruit juice from tall, thin glasses. Sunlight poured in from the big windows. When I'd told my uncle about burning down the garden shed, he'd laughed for a long, long time before wiping the tears from his eyes and agreeing that such an excellent story was definitely worth a secret or two in exchange. He just wished, he said, that I had a picture of my dad's face when he saw what remained of the shed. Then he made me swear on my life not to spill a word to anyone, whoever it might be, and told me everything.

"I was mostly in Lima, the capital," he said, "but I had a few days to spare so I did a bit of traveling. The day before I came home, I was staying in a small town in the Andes, miles from anywhere. In the afternoon, pottering about, as you do, I stumbled across a junk shop. Sitting on the shelf behind the counter was a silver necklace. Very simple, very pretty. The guy could see I was a gringo, so he tried to charge me two hundred dollars. I offered forty and he bargained me up to seventy. That was still way too much, but I needed a present for a girl, so I handed over the cash."

I had a couple of questions—what's a gringo, for instance?—but Uncle Harvey didn't give me a chance to ask anything.

"The necklace was wrapped in a piece of paper," he continued. "I didn't really look at it. I just stuffed it in my pocket and hurried back to the hotel. Next morning, I had an early start. I packed the necklace in the bottom of my suitcase, and that's where it stayed till I came home. In the evening I had a date with that girl. I dug out the necklace. I'd stuffed it in a sock, still wrapped up. I was just about to throw the paper away, but something caught my attention, I don't know what. Call it instinct, call it luck, call it whatever you want, but I happened to notice one of the words on the paper was written in English. As soon as I saw that, I sat down and started working out what it said."

He opened a blue folder and took out a single sheet of crinkly, browned paper.

"Here it is. This is what I found." Uncle Harvey wiped the table with his sleeve and laid the paper carefully in front of me.

It was covered in black marks. Leaning down and looking at them, I realized they were letters. Words. Sentences. So tightly packed and squiggly that every one was an effort to decipher. At the bottom of the page there were two tiny sketches: a gull and a flower. I inspected them for a second, then pored over the spiky writing.

This is what I read:

12th.   This daie we went ashore and toke stoke of muche fine fruit, no one knows the name. We procured wode too.

13th.   Sailed Northwards.

14th.   The same corse.

15th.   About three aclock we found a frigate bownd for Panama. She was laden with Spanish clothes and honie and maize and wyne and much gold and more silver, too much for our owne shippes to carry. Our Captayne sent the crew ashore in a pinnace and we tok the frigate and we sailed to the South.

16th.   We came to anchor among some islands. One of them we had visited before, some days earlier, and it was named by our Captayne the Islande of Theeves for the nature of the natives. Here we did land and got a lyttle water. There was not a native to be seen. Our Captayne took the pinnace ashore and I went with hym and six men also, who were sworne by God to be secret in al they saw. Here we buried five chests filled with gold and three more chests filled with silver. We placed them at the Northern tip of the Islande in a line with the

That was where it ended. In midsentence. Just when it was getting interesting. I turned over the page, but there was nothing on the other side. I looked at my uncle. "This is cool."

"I know."

"So what are you going to do when you get to Peru?"

"Go back to that shop and find the man who sold me the necklace."

"Has he got the rest of the pages?"

"I don't know."

"Why don't you call him?"

"I don't know his number. I don't even know his name. That's why I've got to go back there and find him."

I couldn't help laughing. "So this whole thing might be a waste of time?"

Uncle Harvey shrugged. "Life is about risk."

"You can't just fly to Peru because of a piece of paper!"

"That's exactly what your father would say."

"It's what anyone would say."

"Not me."

"But it might be a forgery! Or a joke! Maybe someone wrote this a week ago for a play or a costume party!"

"They didn't."

"How do you know?"

"I've had it tested. I had the same doubts as you, Tom. I thought it couldn't possibly be genuine. But who on earth would fake a piece of old English parchment and place it in a junk shop halfway up a mountain in the middle of the Andes? Would they do that just on the off-chance that an Englishman might happen to wander past? And if so, why? None of it made much sense, but I knew there was something going on here. Something interesting. So I packed it up and sent it to a friend of mine, a professor at Edinburgh University. He has access to all the latest wizardry. Here's what he said . . ."

He reached for his computer, opened it up, fiddled around for a moment, and turned the screen to face me. Then he pushed back his chair and stood up. "I'm going to pack. My flight leaves this evening. Once I've got my stuff together, we'll talk about keys and I'll show you how to work the locks."

He sauntered out of the room, leaving me to read this e-mail:

FROM: Professor Theodore Parker <theo.parker@ed.ac.uk>

TO: Harvey Trelawney <harvey.trelawney@gmail.com>

SUBJECT: Gold & silver

Hi Harv

I've read your parchment and sent it back registered post, but couldn't resist emailing you immediately to tell you my thoughts.

I'd love to know where you got it! But won't ask. Better not to know? Anyway, as promised, I've subjected it to a battery of tests and am happy to report all seems kosher.

Not wanting to bore you with too much detail, I shall simply tell you that this paper was almost certainly written between 4 and 500 years ago. I could have a go at dating it more precisely, but that would be intuition/ guesswork and you probably don't want that.

Of course, there are a couple of provisos that any cautious scientist (i.e., me) should attach to this result.

1st—the tests could be wrong. However, this is very, very unlikely. One test could certainly be wrong, maybe even two, but I've done all available and they won't all be duds.

2nd—someone might be fooling you. Improbable but not impossible. But let me tell you one thing: if this is a forgery, it's pretty much the most sophisticated I've ever seen.

I could make a few wild guesses about the writer. Young, male, educated. But that would not be scientific and so I'll leave all such speculation to you.

Hope this is useful.

Call me when you're next up here and we'll sink a few jars.

Theo

I closed the computer and put the piece of paper back in the blue folder and realized that there was one terrible problem about my week of freedom in the big city. I didn't want it. If I stayed here I'd spend the whole time wishing I were somewhere else.

I went to the next room. A suitcase was open on the bed. Clothes were scattered everywhere. My uncle was kneeling on the floor, sorting through shoes.

"Uncle Harvey?" I said.

"Please don't call me that."

"Why not?"

"Because it makes me sound like a character in an Enid Blyton novel."

"Oh. Sorry. What should I call you?"

"How about Harvey? That is my name, after all."

"Um, Harvey, can I ask you a question?"

"You can ask me whatever you like." He picked up a sandal and a sneaker, then discarded them both and threw a pair of flip-flops into his suitcase.

"Can I come with you?"

"Where?"

"Peru."

Uncle Harvey shook his head. "I'm sorry, Tom. That's just not possible."

"Why not?"

"Because I'm going alone."

"That's not a reason."

"How about this then: I *want* to go alone."

"You'd have more fun with me, Uncle Harvey."

"Don't call me that."

"Sorry. But it's true. Can't I come too? Please? I've always wanted to go to South America."

"Even if I wanted you to come with me, which I don't, there's one very good reason why you can't. You don't have a ticket."

"I could buy one."

"Or a passport."

"Yes I do. Dad made me bring it in case you weren't here and they had to take me to Nassau."

Uncle Harvey sighed. "Look, Tom. You seem like a very nice kid, and I'm sure we'd have a wonderful time together. If I was going on holiday I'd take you. I really would. But this isn't a holiday. I have enemies in South America. Bad things might happen. Stay here, Tom. Explore the city. You'll have a wild time. We'll go traveling together another year, all right?"

You might think I was dumb to argue. You might be saying to yourself, *What's wrong with this guy? Who wouldn't want a week alone in an apartment in New York City? Without parents. Without teachers. Without his irritating little brother or his know-it-all older sister. Why didn't he just shut up and take the keys and have the best week of his life?*

Well, I thought all that too. And then I thought: *Gold*

and silver. Buried. On an island. In Peru. That's where I want to be. That's what I want to see.

I pleaded and cajoled and begged, but my uncle kept saying no.

I said I'd pay for the flight myself, but he just laughed, which was fair enough. I only had twenty dollars in the world, and that was what Dad had given me to last a whole week in New York.

I promised to be helpful and useful and worth taking too, but he shook his head and said he was quite sure that he'd rather be alone.

I said he couldn't leave me here, because I was too young. It was illegal. What if Social Services found out? They'd call the police, who would arrest Uncle Harvey and throw him in jail for child abuse.

That was when he started looking worried.

I spoke in the deep voice of a TV newscaster: "Now we're going live to New York City, where our correspondent can give us more details about the evil British uncle who left his nephew to rot all alone in a top-floor apartment."

"That's not funny," said Uncle Harvey.

"Look on the bright side," I said. "You'll be famous."

"Don't be ridiculous."

"You'll be on the front page of every newspaper in the country."

"Oh, stop it."

"They'll have your mug shot," I said. "You know, the

one that the police take after you've spent a night in the cell, when you're looking unshaven and dirty and very, very guilty."

"Don't try to blackmail me," said Uncle Harvey. "There's no point. You are not coming with me, and that's final."

3

New York to Lima is about 3,500 miles. We did it in twelve hours. An hour in a taxi to JFK, an hour getting through security, two hours waiting in the departure lounge, and eight hours on the plane.

Have you ever been on an eight-hour flight?

If you haven't, don't bother. It's miserable from start to finish.

Sure, you get free meals, but they're gross, and you get a console attached to the seat with about five hundred different movies, but you don't want to watch any of them because you're so desperate to go to sleep, but you can't get to sleep because the seats are so uncomfortable, so you spend the whole night shuffling and groaning and twisting and turning, and then, when you finally drop off, they switch on the lights and wake you up, and you don't know where you are or what time it is. Then you look at your uncle and you realize he's still snoozing like a baby, because he has a blanket over his knees and an inflatable pillow wrapped around his neck and earplugs in his ears and a mask covering his eyes, and you think: *Why didn't he offer all that stuff to me?*

I sat beside him, crammed into my seat, wriggling and fiddling, trying to get comfortable. When I wasn't watching movies or attempting to sleep, I read *Lonely Planet: Peru.* I'd persuaded Uncle Harvey to buy me a copy at the airport. He told me it wasn't worth it. He said guidebooks were for wimps. But I wanted to know some basic information about where we were going.

Peru is twice the size of Texas. Did you know that? And it's one of the most diverse countries in the world. It has mountains, desert, *and* tropical jungle. Plus a coastline that is 1,500 miles long.

Today was Tuesday. We'd arrive in Lima on Wednesday morning. Our flights home left next Monday night, arriving in New York on Tuesday—giving me just enough time to race back to Uncle Harvey's apartment, open the door to Mom and Dad, and compliment them on their tans.

We had five full days in Peru. Five days to search 1,500 miles of coastline and find the Island of Thieves. Oh, and we didn't have a plan.

Five days, 1,500 miles, and no plan. What could possibly go wrong?

Uncle Harvey finally woke up when the plane landed. He pulled off his eye mask, plucked out his earplugs, and stretched his arms. "Ahhhh! I'm ready for a huge breakfast. How about you, Tommy-boy? Are you hungry?"

"I've had breakfast already. They gave us some about an hour ago."

"Was it disgusting?"

"Yes, it was, actually."

"Then you deserve another. We'll go to the Café Florés. It's one of the few places in Lima that serve a decent cup of coffee."

"I don't like coffee."

"Why not?"

"I don't know. I just don't like the taste."

"How perverse. Oh, well. They do good toasted sand-wiches, too. Or maybe you'd like to try the national dish of Peru?"

"Sure," I said. "What is it?"

"Guinea pig and chips."

"Yeah, right."

"I'm not joking," said Uncle Harvey. "You can't leave Peru without tasting their national dish. They take a guinea pig, chop him in half, open him out, and fry him on a griddle. Delicious! But I suppose it's not the best thing for breakfast. We'll try some tonight."

"No way," I said. "I am not eating guinea pig."

Uncle Harvey just smiled, that same irritating smile, the one that said: *I know more than you do.* I could see he was quite confident that by the end of the week I would have eaten a guinea pig. And asked for seconds.

We had to wait about an hour to go through passport

control, then about another to collect our luggage. I said, "Why is this taking so long?"

"Welcome to South America," replied Uncle Harvey.

When we finally had both our bags, we wheeled them into the corridor marked NOTHING TO DECLARE. Uniformed guards watched us through dark glasses.

On the other side of customs, we emerged in the main part of the airport. Taxi drivers surrounded us, waving their arms and shouting in a mixture of Spanish and English. Uncle Harvey shoved them aside and marched toward the car rental desks. I hurried after him. No one tried to grab my bag or tempt me into a taxi. I suppose they knew I wasn't worth bothering with. It was obvious I didn't have any money.

Uncle Harvey hadn't booked a car in advance. He said they're cheaper if you just show up and bargain. We joined the line and shuffled slowly forward, watching people ahead of us hand over their passports and driving licenses.

We were almost at the front of the line—just one more couple between us and the desk—when a man in a dark suit sidled up to my uncle and said, "Meester Arveee Trelaw-wneee?"

(He really did speak like that, but I'm not going to write down his crazy accent all the way through. You'll just have to imagine it for yourself.)

Uncle Harvey said, "Who are you?"

"My name is Ricardo Cassinelli. Could you come with me, please? My car is waiting outside."

"I'm not going anywhere with you," said my uncle. "I don't know who you are."

"I am the representative of someone who wishes to speak with you."

"Who?"

"I would rather not say. But I can tell you, Mr. Trelawney, he is a good friend of yours."

"You've got me confused with someone else," said my uncle. "I don't have any friends in Peru. Now if you'll excuse me, I have to pick up my rental."

Uncle Harvey tried to move away, but Ricardo gripped his arm. He leaned in and spoke quietly into my uncle's ear. I don't know what he said, but his words had an obvious impact: for the first time since I'd been with him, my uncle looked worried. It didn't last long. A nervous expression flashed across his features for only a brief moment and then he was back to normal, smiling as if everything was fine. I was intrigued. What had Ricardo said? Had he whispered a threat? What was it?

The couple in front of us had signed their paperwork and collected the key for their car. It was our turn. I pushed my bag along the floor. Uncle Harvey tried to do the same, but Ricardo was still holding his arm in a firm grip.

I noticed a couple of other men lingering nearby. They had broad shoulders and enormous, hairy hands. From the way they were watching us, I realized they were with Ricardo, providing him with some backup in case we tried to run away or fight.

"Can I help you?" said the guy behind the desk.

My uncle glanced at the car rental guy, then at me, and then at the people behind us in line. He gave them one of his most charming smiles. "I'm terribly sorry," he said. "Why don't you go ahead of us?"

They approached the desk and showed their passports to the clerk. Uncle Harvey stepped aside and I followed him. There was a muttered conversation between my uncle and Ricardo. I couldn't hear what either of them said, but Ricardo must have been very persuasive, because my uncle turned to me and said in a low voice, "I'm sorry about this, Tom. I've got to go and see someone. It won't take long. These guys will give me a lift into the center of town and then I'll come back here and pick you up. You can look after yourself, can't you?"

I didn't like the idea of staying in the airport on my own, particularly since I had only twenty dollars and no clue what that might be worth in Peruvian money, but I didn't want to complain. I just nodded. "No problem."

"Great. Thank you. Find a café. Read a book. I'll be back soon. If there's any problem, you've got my number, haven't you?"

"I don't know if my phone will work here."

"Of course it will. You'll be fine. See you later." Uncle Harvey turned to Ricardo. "Let's go."

"He comes too," said Ricardo, pointing at me.

"No, he doesn't," said Uncle Harvey. "He's staying here."

"He comes too," repeated Ricardo.

"This is nothing to do with him. He's just a kid who I met on the flight. We were sitting next to one another. I said I'd give him a lift into Lima."

Ricardo smiled. "But he has the same name as you."

"Does he? That's a coincidence."

"I think he is your nephew."

Now Uncle Harvey smiled too. There was no point pretending. Whoever they were, they already knew everything about us. "You're right, he's my nephew, but he doesn't know the first thing about me or my business. There's no need for him to come with us."

"Is no problem," said Ricardo. He nodded to the two thugs, who relieved us of our bags.

I wanted to know who we were going to see and why, but there wasn't a chance to ask any questions. Ricardo led my uncle through the airport. I hurried after them. The thugs followed behind, bringing the bags.

I could have run away. I'm pretty sure I would have made it. Ricardo and the two thugs would have stayed with Uncle Harvey, making sure he didn't escape. They weren't really interested in me.

But if I ran away, I'd be all alone. A kid in a foreign country with no money, no friends, and nowhere to go. I'd be much safer, I decided, if I stayed with my uncle.

Which shows how much I knew.

4

Outside the main entrance to the airport, an enormous, gleaming black Mercedes was parked in the zone that said NO PARKING. I thought it must belong to the president or a pop star, but it was actually waiting for us. The chauffeur was wearing a peaked cap and a smart uniform with lots of shiny buttons. He opened the back door and smiled at my uncle. *"Buenos días,* Señor Trelawney. Welcome to Peru."

We got inside. So did Ricardo.

Another Mercedes rolled up behind ours. The thugs got in that one with our luggage. We drove out of the airport and headed for Lima.

The journey took about half an hour. During that time, no one said a word. I kept glancing at my uncle, expecting him to explain everything, but he stared straight ahead, watching the view out the windshield, lost in his own thoughts. He didn't even bother smiling at me or giving me a friendly look to say, *Don't worry, Tom. Everything's going to be fine.*

I had spent less than twenty-four hours with Uncle Harvey, but I was already beginning to appreciate why he and my dad didn't see each other more often.

My dad . . . he's a nice guy. No doubt about that. Everyone says so. He's not exactly exciting, though. I don't mean that in a bad way. He'd be the first to admit it. "All I want is a quiet life"—that's one of his favorite sayings. I don't think he's ever been in trouble. When he has to come to my school and listen to my teachers explaining why they've given me yet another detention, he always has the same expression on his face, a mixture of disappointment and astonishment, as if he simply can't understand why anyone would even *want* to disobey his teachers.

My uncle is quite different. I could see that already.

Of course, I didn't yet realize *how* different.

In the center of the city we parked outside a large apartment block right by the beach. *Hey,* I thought, *look! There's the Pacific! The biggest ocean on the planet! Is that cool, or what?* I looked at Uncle Harvey and Ricardo, expecting them to be excited too, but of course they'd seen it all before.

We climbed out of the car and Ricardo had a word with the chauffeur. The two thugs stood nearby, clutching our bags. I took the chance to ask my uncle in a quiet voice: "What's all this about?"

"We're going to see someone. It won't take long."

"Who are we going to see?"

"A nasty piece of work called Otto Gonzalez. I'll tell

you all about him later." By now, Ricardo was coming back again. Uncle Harvey barely had time to whisper, "Don't say too much, OK? Just keep smiling." Then he was hurrying forward. "So, where's Otto?"

"Upstairs," said Ricardo. "Please, follow me."

We went inside. On the ground floor there was a huge lobby with potted plants and mirrors and a marble floor and two security guards sitting behind a desk. They nodded at Ricardo. One of them must have pressed a button under the desk, because the elevator doors slid open.

We went up to the top floor. The penthouse. Through a big wooden door into a long hallway lined with paintings. "This way, please," said Ricardo. He led us into a massive room with big windows overlooking the sea. A man and a woman were sitting at a long table, a platter of croissants between them. There were several other men in the room too, leaning against the walls or lounging in chairs. One of them had a pistol tucked into his belt. They looked like bodyguards or servants, while the couple eating breakfast were the boss and his wife. That's what I would have guessed, anyway, and it turned out I was right.

Otto Gonzalez was a small man, but he was solid and square, a little block of muscle. I hardly even looked at his face; all my attention was drawn to the extraordinary tattoo on his neck: the head of a snake, its mouth open, its fangs raised, snarling under his chin. Otto's white shirt was un-buttoned just enough to show a few loops of the snake's tail crisscrossing his thick, hairy chest. For all I knew, the rest of the snake curled all around his body, even down his legs and up again.

His wife was skinny, blond, and very beautiful. She didn't have any tattoos. Or hair on her chest. She looked like a model and must have been half his age.

"Harvey Trelawney," said Otto, wiping his mouth with his napkin. "This is a surprise, huh?"

"A nice surprise, I hope," said my uncle, smiling as if he were greeting an old friend. "It's good to see you."

"Don't speak so soon," said Otto. His English was pretty good, although he had a strange accent, half American and half Spanish. "I have to tell you, Harvey, I am not happy with you. You have cheated me, my friend."

"What on earth are you talking about?"

"You know what I'm talking about, Harvey."

"Actually, I don't."

"Oh, really? You don't? Then why do you think I want to see you?"

"I'm very much hoping it's because you want to buy another picture."

"Another picture?" Otto's face flushed with blood, and he rose out of his chair. "Are you joking me?"

"I thought you liked the first one."

"I like it till I find it's a fake!"

"Fake?" My uncle sounded astonished. "What do you mean?"

Otto issued a quick order to one of his men, who hurried out of the room and returned a moment later with a painting in a gold frame.

I don't know much about art, but I know what I don't like, and I didn't like this. I think it was supposed to be a picture of a woman sitting in a chair, but she was all distorted and multicolored and kind of a mess. I could have done better with my eyes shut.

My uncle ogled the picture as if he'd never set eyes on anything so lovely. "It's a wonderful piece of work, isn't it?"

"Wonderful? You think this is wonderful?"

"I certainly do."

"Then you're crazy. Or you're lying. I don't know which." Otto gave the wooden frame a dismissive flick with his fingers. "I bring a man all the way from New York to see this picture. I tell him, 'I got a picture, I think it's worth ten million dollars.' You know what he say to me? He say, it's worth nothing. Nothing! You cheat me, Harvey. You say you're sure it's Picasso."

"I was sure it was," said my uncle. "If it's not, that's my mistake, and I'm very sorry. But it's still a lovely picture, isn't it? I'm sure you'll enjoy it very much for years to come."

"I don't want to enjoy it. I want my money back."

"That's really not possible, Otto. I told you that I couldn't give you any guarantees. That's why this picture was so cheap. If you'd bought it through a dealer in London or New York, it would have cost you six or seven million dollars."

"But it would have been real!"

"That's true," said my uncle. "But life is about risk, isn't it? You took a risk, and this time it didn't work out. I'm sure we'll have a better experience when we next do business together."

That was when Otto's expression changed. His smile faded and his eyes darkened. For the first time since they started arguing, I began to feel seriously nervous. Up until now, I'd accepted Uncle Harvey's own view of the situation; he'd seemed utterly confident and so I was too. Now I wasn't sure. What had we walked into? And would we be able to get out of here? I looked at the door, but it was blocked by two big men with broad shoulders. The only other exit was the door onto the terrace, and I didn't like that: a long drop followed by falling facefirst into the biggest ocean on the planet.

"Give me my money," said Otto. His voice was lower, deeper, darker. He sounded like a gangster in a movie. I wondered if he'd learned his English from watching *The Godfather* and *The Sopranos,* and then I wondered if the actors in *The Godfather* and *The Sopranos* had learned their parts by watching men like him.

Uncle Harvey didn't seem too bothered. He was still managing to look calm and relaxed, smiling as if he didn't have a care in the world. I wondered what he knew that I didn't, or if he was just really good at bluffing. "I'm terribly sorry," he said. "I wish I could give you back all your money, but I simply can't."

"Why not?" growled Otto.

"I don't have it."

"You better get it. I want one hundred thousand dollars."

"I really don't have access to that kind of cash at the moment. If you could hang on for five or six months, I might be able to—"

"I'm not gonna wait six months. I want my money now."

"I'll tell you what," said Uncle Harvey. "I'm a business-man. I don't like unhappy customers. If you really don't want this picture, I'll buy it back from you. Of course, I'll need a little time to raise the cash. Why don't you give me a couple of weeks and I'll see what I can do?"

"You got twenty-four hours," said Otto.

"That's simply not possible," said Uncle Harvey.

"Everything is possible."

There was something ominous about the way Otto said those words. What happened next was even worse. He ordered his wife to leave the room. She sulkily gathered up her coffee and her newspaper and stalked out. Once she had gone and the door was closed, Otto told two of his men to take hold of Uncle Harvey's arms. No one touched me; they seemed to have forgotten that I even existed.

Otto walked to the sideboard, opened a drawer, and pulled out a long carving knife. Uncle Harvey struggled, but the thugs were too strong for him. They sat him in a chair and spread his hand out on the table.

As soon as I realized what was happening, I threw myself toward my uncle, trying to dislodge the men who were holding him. But I wasn't quick enough. One of the thugs grabbed me and held me back.

Otto was smiling. He ran his finger slowly along the blade.

"Which finger you wanna lose?" he said to my uncle. "If it is me, I say the little one. But you can choose. The left hand? The right hand? The big finger? The little finger? Which you want?"

Uncle Harvey thought for a moment. I could see him considering it: The left or the right? Which would be less useful? What could he live without more easily? And then he said, "I might be able to get your money a bit quicker."

"You see?" said Otto. "Like I say before. Everything is possible."

"Give me a week."

Otto shook his head. "One day. Twenty-four hours. Starting now." He glanced at the clock. "You better get going, Harvey. Tick-tock. Tick-tock. Tick-tock."

"Very well," said Uncle Harvey. "I'll have the money for you in twenty-four hours. But you're going to have to let me go. I can't do it from here. I have to make some calls and meet some people."

"Sure, no problem."

Otto nodded to his men, who stepped back, letting my uncle go.

He stood up, rubbing his wrist.

"You come back here," said Otto. "Same time tomorrow. You have my money. And you take away your picture."

"It's a deal," my uncle said, and then nodded to me. "Let's go, Tom."

Before I could move, Otto said, "He stays here."

"That wasn't the deal."

"It is now," said Otto. "Come back here in twenty-four hours with the money. Then you can have him."

"No chance," said Uncle Harvey.

"Is no problem." Otto looked at me. "You like computers? You like games? You wanna stay here and play some games?"

Suddenly everyone was looking at me. I smiled, trying to look as cool as Uncle Harvey. "Sure," I said. "I love games." I turned to my uncle. "I don't mind staying here. Seriously, Uncle Harvey, I'll be fine."

My uncle gave a little shake of his head. I could see him mulling over the situation, thinking through his options and considering what to do. He didn't take long to reach a decision. He pulled back his chair and sat down again. "Listen, Otto. Let me tell you why I'm in Peru."

"I don't care why you're in Peru," said Otto. "One hundred thousand dollars, that's all I want."

"Let me tell you anyway," said my uncle.

He started talking. At first Otto made it quite clear that he wasn't even listening, pouring himself another cup of coffee and walking around the room, but Uncle Harvey just kept talking and gradually managed to get Otto's attention, telling him about the necklace and the shop in the mountains, just as he had told me. He avoided giving any specific information about the shop's location, dodging Otto's questions by opening his bag, taking out his blue folder, and handing over the old, crumpled piece of paper.

Otto stared at it for a long time. I don't know why. I'm sure he couldn't read the handwriting. I found it hard enough and I speak English.

"There are no guarantees," said my uncle. "But I think it's a risk worth taking. That's why I've come back to Peru. I'm going to start searching for this treasure today. If I find it, my first stop will be right here. I'm going to give you a lump of gold worth a hundred thousand dollars."

"That's a good story," said Otto. "I just got one question. Is it true?"

"Of course it's true."

"You sure? Because I'm thinking, Harvey, maybe you're not very good at telling the truth."

"I swear on my life," said my uncle.

Otto pointed at me. "You swear on his life?"

Uncle Harvey nodded without even pausing to think. "I swear on his life too. Every word is true."

Otto reached across the table and opened a box of thin cigars. He offered one to my uncle, then to me, but we both said no. He lit one, leaned back in his chair, and blew smoke at the ceiling. He was smiling. It was difficult to believe that only a few minutes ago he'd been threatening to chop off my uncle's little finger. He asked a few more questions, getting the details straight in his mind, and then he said, "You know what, Harvey? We'll do this thing together. You and me, we'll find the island and the treasure too. What do you say? It'll be fun, no?"

"That's a very nice offer," said Uncle Harvey. From his tone of voice, I couldn't tell whether he was genuinely interested or just humoring our host. "If you don't mind me asking, how exactly are you going to help us? What can you do that we can't?"

Otto gave him a little smile as if he were a child who had asked a silly question. "To come to this island, you must have a boat. To find the treasure, you need men. You are an Englishman, Harvey, but this is my country. I have men. I have cars. I have planes and helicopters. I have boats. Together we can do everything. And when we find the treasure, we will split it between us, half for you and half for me. That is fair, no?"

"I'm not sure that's very fair at all," said Uncle Harvey. "How about eighty-twenty?"

Otto shook his head. "Half-half."

"Seventy-thirty."

"Half-half."

"Sixty-forty."

"Half-half."

"Let me get one thing straight. For that price, you'll supply whatever we need? Equipment, men, boats, cars—everything?"

"Everything," said Otto.

Uncle Harvey thought for a moment, considering his options. Then he nodded. "It's always a pleasure doing business with you, Otto. You've got yourself a deal."

5

Suddenly everyone was smiling. Otto rubbed his hands together. "Let's have a drink! What do you want, Harvey? A whiskey?"

"That's very kind of you, Otto, but I can't possibly drink at this time of the morning. I haven't even had breakfast."

"That's no problem! Have a whiskey for breakfast!"

"If you don't mind, I'd rather have a hot shower and a decent cup of coffee. Would that be possible?"

"Sure, no problem—we got showers, we got coffee, we got whatever you want. Maria will show you to a room."

Maria was the maid, a skinny girl in a black dress. Otto issued an order to her in Spanish. He must have been telling her which rooms to put us in.

"You should have a shower too," my uncle said to me.

I said I was fine, but my uncle insisted. I guess I must have smelled.

Maria led us down the corridor. I had a bunch of questions for my uncle. I wanted to know what was going to happen to me. Was I staying here or going with him? Plus, what if we couldn't find the treasure? What if it had already been found by someone else? If the island had been turned into a resort and a huge hotel had been built on the exact spot where the treasure was hidden, would he still owe Otto a hundred thousand dollars? But I didn't get a chance to ask any of these questions. As soon as I started talking, my uncle put his finger to his lips and nodded at the maid.

She showed us to our rooms. I went into mine and shut the door. It was massive—three times the size of my room at home, if not bigger. And there I have to share the bathroom with Mom, Dad, Grace, and Jack, whereas here I had my own private bathroom with an enormous bath and gold taps and a thick, fluffy white robe hanging on the back of the door.

I stood by the window, looking at the view of the ocean, and wondered what to do next. I was in a whole heap of trouble, that much was obvious. Had I made a huge mistake coming here? Should I have stayed in New York?

Stop worrying, I told myself. *Trust Uncle Harvey. He knows what he's doing. Have a shower, like he told you, and see what happens next.*

My bag was on the bed. It must have been put there by one of the maids. I pulled off my sweater and slipped off my shoes. I was just about to step out of my jeans when the door opened. It was my uncle.

"You could knock," I said.

He closed the door before answering.

"Get your stuff together," he said in a whisper. "We're leaving."

"Now?"

"Shhh!" He put his finger to his lips. "We've got to get out of here. Come on."

"Where are we going?"

"Anywhere. Just not here. As you've probably realized already, Otto Gonzalez is one of the biggest crooks in South America. I'll tell you the gory details later, but now we've got to hurry. Didn't I tell you to put your shoes on?"

"Wait a minute," I said. "You've just made a deal with the biggest crook in South America and now you're going to double-cross him? Are you crazy?"

"We don't have any choice. If we stick around, Otto will kill us."

"Then why did you—"

My uncle interrupted me: "I'm leaving. You can stay here if you want to. Your choice."

I pulled on my sneakers, put my sweater back on, and grabbed my bag. Uncle Harvey opened the door and tiptoed into the corridor. He glanced both ways. From the other end of the apartment, we could hear music and conversation. Uncle Harvey nodded to me and walked quickly and quietly toward the big wooden door of the apartment. I hurried after him.

A floorboard creaked. We stopped and listened. Seconds

passed. There were no more creaks. Uncle Harvey nodded and we kept walking.

Everything went fine till we got to the main door. There, sitting on a chair, reading a newspaper, was one of Otto's men. I suppose he was making sure we didn't do exactly what we were doing. When he saw us he stood up, dropped his newspaper on the chair, and positioned himself solidly in front of the door. He must have noticed that we were carrying our bags, but he didn't say anything, just waited for us to make the first move.

I looked at my uncle, wondering how he was going to talk his way out of this situation. I'm sure I must have looked terrified, but my uncle appeared as cool as always. He stepped forward with a cheerful grin on his face and said, "Hello, Miguel. It is Miguel, isn't it?" He paused for a moment, giving the man a chance to answer, then realized the guy wasn't going to and hurried onward: "We're just heading out for a moment. Could we get past, please?"

Miguel replied in Spanish.

Uncle Harvey stuck to English: "Don't be difficult, Miguel. Señor Gonzalez has asked me to fetch something and I'm sure he doesn't want to be kept waiting. Excuse me, please." He tried to step past, but Miguel wouldn't budge. He was a big man with broad shoulders and there was no way around him.

If I had been in Uncle Harvey's position, I don't know what I would have done. Apologized, probably. Then gone back to my room and tried to think of a good lie to tell Otto.

Uncle Harvey had his own way of doing things. He dropped his bag on the floor, swung his arm, and threw a punch.

I was impressed. If you met him, you wouldn't immediately think that Uncle Harvey was the type of guy who could take care of himself in a fight, but he had a neat right hook. His arm whipped through the air and his fist rammed into Miguel's chin with a very satisfying crunch.

A punch like that—it would have been enough to knock me across the room. Most men would have fallen to the ground, clutching their broken chins and seeing stars. Not Miguel. He barely flinched.

The momentum of the punch put my uncle off-balance. Before he could right himself, he had been grabbed by Miguel, who whirled him around in one crisp movement and bent him over with his right arm twisted up behind his back.

"Arrrggghh!" yelled my uncle.

Miguel shouted loudly in Spanish. I didn't know what he was saying, but he must have been calling for help.

No one answered.

He shouted again, louder.

My uncle tried to free himself and then cried out once more as Miguel jerked his arm upward. A little further and the bone would have snapped. Uncle Harvey must have known that, but he didn't stop struggling, and he kicked backwards with one heel, then the other, trying to connect with Miguel's ankles.

And me? What was I doing?

Standing there like an idiot. Just watching. As if these two guys were a couple of wrestlers on TV, not my uncle and some thug.

I knew I had to do something.

But what?

On a sideboard there was a tall vase decorated with blue and white flowers. I picked it up with both hands, swung it through the air and brought it crashing down on Miguel's head.

The vase smashed into a thousand pieces.

Miguel gave a funny little groan and fell facefirst on the carpet.

Uncle Harvey was at the door immediately, pulling back the bolt. I picked up his bag as well as mine. His was heavy, but I didn't seem to feel its weight. We ran into the corridor. The elevator was right ahead of us. Uncle Harvey pressed the button. We were lucky; it was there. The doors slid open. We stepped inside and headed for the ground floor.

6

In my uncle's eyes, I could see a glimmer of respect that hadn't been there before. "Nice work with the vase, kiddo. Where did you learn to do that?"

"From movies, I guess."

"You must have been watching some good movies. Once we get out of here, you'll have to tell me the titles. Now, when the door opens and we step into the lobby, don't start running. Wait till we reach the street. Do you understand?"

"Sure."

We sauntered out of the elevator like two guys without a care in the world. Uncle Harvey nodded to the security guards, who nodded back. We walked through the door and onto the pavement. Once we were out of sight of the guards, my uncle yelled, "Go!"

We sprinted down the street, swerving past surprised pedestrians. My bag clonked against a man's knee. I hoped he wouldn't come after us too. We turned a corner, then another, leaving the sea and Otto's apartment building far behind us.

I could have kept running, but my uncle waved at me to stop. He was doubled over, red-faced, gasping for breath.

I looked back along the street. No one was running toward us.

I said, "Do you think they'll come after us?"

My uncle straightened up, still panting, and nodded. "Otto will be furious. He'll comb the entire country till he finds us."

"What are we going to do?"

"Get in that cab." He stepped off the pavement and waved his arm. A taxi on the other side of the street did a neat U-turn and came to pick us up.

As we drove quickly through Lima, Uncle Harvey told me what he knew about Otto Gonzalez. "He's a major criminal. His networks run drugs out of Peru and into Colombia and Mexico, and from there to the U.S. He's famous for torturing his enemies before killing them, and over the course of his long and crooked career, he's apparently committed several hundred murders."

"But you sold him a picture."

"I needed the money."

"Couldn't you pay him back?"

"Sadly, no."

"Why not?"

"Why do you think, Tom? I've already spent it."

"A hundred thousand dollars?" I said. "What did you spend it on?"

"Quite a lot went on your plane ticket."

It was true: my ticket had been darn expensive. Yesterday, when we'd checked on the Internet, there was only one seat left on the flight and it cost $2,200. Which was more money than I'd ever had in my entire life. At the time, Uncle Harvey had told me not to worry and whipped out his credit card. I could pay him back, he'd said, when we found the gold.

"I know twenty-two hundred dollars is a ton of money," I said. "But even that would leave a lot of change from a hundred thousand dollars. What did you spend the rest on?"

"Mostly paying the guy who did the painting."

At first, I didn't understand what he was talking about. When I did, I managed to stammer, "You sell fake paintings?"

"I do all kinds of things," said Uncle Harvey.

"Like what, exactly?"

"A bit of this and a bit of that."

"What does that mean? What do you actually *do?*"

"When we know one another a bit better, I'll tell you. But not now. Sorry, Tom. It's probably safer if you don't know everything about me."

"You don't have to tell me everything," I said. "But you can tell me this, at least. If you knew you'd sold a fake painting to a ruthless murderer, why did you come back to his country? Shouldn't you have stayed out of Peru for the rest of your life?"

"That would have been very sensible." Uncle Harvey

grinned in that irritating way of his, and I thought he was about to say something rude about my dad. "If you recall, Tom, I tried to persuade you to stay in New York, but you bullied and blackmailed me into changing my mind. So don't try to make me feel guilty. And, whatever you do, don't blame me for bringing you here."

"I didn't know I was going to be chased around the country by a bloodthirsty criminal."

"If you had, would you have stayed at home?"

I didn't even have to think about that. "No."

"So stop complaining. Now relax. Otto will never find us. We're much too cunning for him. We're Trelawneys, remember? We're used to trouble. It's in our genes. Don't worry, Tom. Everything's going to be fine."

I didn't believe him for a moment. I wondered if he even believed himself. Or was he just trying to make me feel better? And what did he mean about our having trouble in our genes? As far as I knew, I came from a long line of shopkeepers and bank managers. That was what Dad had told me, anyway. But now wasn't the time for a family history lesson. I had a far more important question for my uncle: "If Otto's such a big crook, why isn't he hiding? How can he live in the middle of the city? With a tattoo like that, he's not exactly invisible. Why don't the police arrest him?"

"The police only arrest little criminals," said Uncle Harvey. "They can't touch the big ones."

"Why not?"

"That's just the way the world works."

"What do you mean?"

"Haven't you ever heard of bribery and corruption?"

"He pays them?"

"Of course! Otto slips the chief of police a few million dollars. The cops leave him alone. Simple as that."

The taxi stopped outside a high-rise apartment building. We retrieved our bags and went inside. A porter in a peaked cap was slouched behind a long wooden desk, half asleep, a crumpled newspaper on his lap. The sound of the door woke him up. He gave a funny little salute. "*Buenos días,* Señor Harvey."

"*Buenos días,* Felipe."

Felipe led us across the hallway and ushered us into the elevator. He pressed the button marked eight and dodged out as the doors slid shut.

I said, "Where are we?"

"A friend of mine lives here."

"Who?"

"Just a friend. We're going to borrow her car. If she'll lend it to us. So smile nicely, Tom, and try to look trustworthy."

On the eighth floor, the doors opened and we stepped out into a long corridor lined with a shabby old carpet. Uncle Harvey walked to apartment 83. He rapped his knuckles loudly on the door. A voice came from inside, calling out in Spanish, and then the door was opened by a tall woman with long black hair. She was wearing a white bathrobe and a pair of pink flip-flops. She stared at my uncle as if she couldn't believe her big black eyes. "Arvee? Is it really you?"

"Hello, Alejandra." My uncle darted in and kissed her three times, once on each cheek and then once more on the lips.

Her name, by the way, was pronounced Allay-handra. I didn't know the spelling till later. Apparently it's the same name as Alexandra in English.

"I want you to meet someone." Uncle Harvey brought me forward. "May I present my nephew, Tom Trelawney."

Alejandra smiled at me. She had gleaming white teeth. "I am happy for meeting you, Tom." She placed her thin hand in mine. I could feel the bones through her skin. "My name is Alejandra Catalina, and I am a friend of Arvee. Welcome in Lima. Please, you will enter?"

Compared to Otto's magnificent apartment, Alejandra's apartment was like a cupboard. There were just two main rooms, a bedroom and a kitchen, plus a tiny, cramped bathroom. If you sat on the toilet, your knees jammed against the bath. It was cozy, though. I slumped on a sofa and thought, *Yes, this is nice—I wouldn't mind staying here for a couple of days.*

Of course, we couldn't. I knew that already. We'd told Otto much too much about our plans. His thugs would be out looking for us. The police, too. All the people that he'd bribed. He probably had spies everywhere. They'd be searching the whole city for us. The whole country. Hunting for Harvey Trelawney and his nephew Tom.

7

Alejandra's car was small, red, and smashed to pieces. It looked as if it had been in a fight with a bigger, nastier car and stumbled away, clutching its nose. The body was covered in bumps and scratches. Rust had eaten away at the metal. One of the back windows was cracked. I wondered if it would pass an inspection and then I wondered if they even had inspections in Peru.

Uncle Harvey wasn't complaining, so I kept quiet too. If you're in a strange city and you need a free car, you take whatever you can get. Especially if there's a murderous international criminal on your tail.

Uncle Harvey loaded our bags into the trunk. I wondered if Alejandra would be coming with us, but she kissed me on both cheeks and said, *"Adiós,* Tom."

"Bye. Thanks for the car. We'll bring it back in one piece, I promise."

I don't think she heard me. She'd already turned her attention to Uncle Harvey. I looked the other way. Eventually my uncle freed himself from her clutches and took the key from her hand. We got inside and drove off.

At the end of the street, I looked back. Alejandra was still waving. I glanced at my uncle, wondering if he would wave back, but he didn't seem to notice her. Then we turned the corner and she was gone.

I said, "Is she your girlfriend?"

"Yes and no," replied Uncle Harvey.

"What does that mean? Is she or isn't she?"

"These things are complicated. You'll understand when you're a bit older." He punched his hand on the horn. "Are you blind?"

That last bit was addressed to a car driving toward us on the wrong side of the road. The car didn't change direction, so Uncle Harvey took evasive action, skidding up onto the sidewalk, scattering pedestrians, and then bumping down onto the road again and lurching onward.

As we drove through the city, I searched the faces that we passed, looking out for Ricardo, Miguel, and Otto's other thugs. I didn't see them, but that didn't mean that they—or their friends, or their spies, or their closed circuit cameras—hadn't seen us.

On the outskirts, we passed through miles of slums. Little kids stood by the side of the road, dressed in rags, waving their hands. Some of them were selling sticks of chewing gum or sweets wrapped in foil. Others were just begging for coins. Behind them, I could see their homes, one-room shacks with a single sheet of corrugated iron for a roof and a few old boxes for furniture. I remembered my bedroom and my bike and my computer, and I felt very grateful to have been born when and where I was. I tried to express this to my uncle, but he just laughed.

"Welcome to the world," he said. "Connecticut might not look much like this, but most of the rest of the planet does."

The air cleared as the road climbed. By midday, the gray mist had gone. When the road twisted, I could see for miles down a long valley.

We stopped for lunch at a ramshackle café, where we ate cheese pies and boiled potatoes. Uncle Harvey drank yet another cup of coffee and tried to persuade me to have one too. For about the fourteenth time, I told him I don't like coffee, but he didn't seem to believe me.

Throughout the afternoon, the road got steadily worse. It clung to the edge of a steep hillside and the surface wasn't even paved. Soon we were skidding and scrambling along a muddy path that would have been a farm track at home. Out here, it was the main highway from Lima to the backcountry, the only route for cars, trucks, and buses.

There was no barrier marking the side of the road. If Uncle Harvey lost concentration for a second, we'd slither straight over the edge. If that happened, survival wasn't an option. It would just be a long drop and then the end of everything.

You might think I'm being melodramatic, but we saw

burned-out wrecks of cars and trucks all along the route, smeared over the hillside or lying upside down at the bottom of a valley like dead beetles on a carpet.

My phone beeped. I had a look at the screen. There was a text:

> Hello, darling. How is New York? It's very
> hot and sunny here. We're having a lovely
> time swimming. Loads of love from Mom.

Mom's texts are always like that. Every word spelled out and all the grammar perfect.

I texted back that New York was cool and so was Uncle Harvey and we were having a great time together.

What would Mom and Dad say if they knew where I was right now?

They wouldn't say anything. They'd just jump on a plane and come and get me.

Would I ever tell them where I had really spent this week?

Maybe, maybe not. It might have to stay my little secret forever. Anyway, there was no need to worry about that now. It could wait till I got back to Connecticut. If I ever got back to Connecticut.

I settled back in my seat and stared out the window at the sun dipping behind the snow-tipped mountains. The sky turned a deeper shade of gray. The air was suddenly chilly. Along with the change of weather, the road seemed to be getting even worse, narrower and wetter and more slippery, and I wondered what would happen if we were stuck out here all night.

It was almost dark when we finally arrived on a shabby little street in a shabby little town. The junk shop didn't just look shut; it had the appearance of a place that had closed down many years ago. We got out and peered through the dark windows, but there was no sign of life inside.

Uncle Harvey nodded to a group of men sitting in a café across the street. "Let's ask them where the shopkeeper lives."

He sauntered up to the table. *"Buenos noches."*

"Buenos noches," replied a couple of the men. They were old and toothless. Some of them were drinking beer and others had tiny glasses of some colorless liquid. There was a pile of dominoes on the table.

"We're looking for the guy who owns that shop." Uncle Harvey pointed across the street. "Do you know where he is?"

The old men stared at him blankly. One of them said, *"Inglés?"*

"Sí," said Uncle Harvey. *"Inglés. Hablas Inglés?"*

One of them laughed and the others shook their heads.

"Gracias," said Uncle Harvey. *"Adiós!"*

"Adiós!" they called back, raising their glasses and toasting us.

Uncle Harvey took my arm. "Let's go and find a hotel."

We walked back to the car.

I said, "Why were you talking to them in English?"

"Why not?"

"Don't they speak Spanish?"

"I'm sure they do."

"Then why don't you speak to them in Spanish?"

"Because I can't."

I stared at him like an idiot. "You can't speak Spanish?"

"I can say a few words. *Buenos días. Adiós. Una cerveza, por favor. Dónde está el baño?* But that's about it."

"I don't believe this," I said. "We've come treasure-hunting in Peru and you can't even speak Spanish!"

"I don't know why you're so surprised," said Uncle Harvey. "We've been here for a whole day. Have you heard me speak a single word of the local lingo?"

Thinking about it, I realized he had indeed been talking to everyone in English. Like an idiot, I'd assumed he was doing it for *my* benefit.

"This is crazy," I said. "How are we ever going to find this treasure if you can't even speak their language?"

"We'll be fine," replied Uncle Harvey. "Stop worrying. Now get in the car. I think I saw a sign for a hotel on the road into town."

You know, I felt like saying, *I'm meant to be the doofus here. You're the adult. You're twice my age. No: three times. You are three times my age, Uncle Harvey, and you've brought me to Peru to hunt for buried treasure and you've offended a major criminal and he's going to track us down and kill us, and now we're in a little town miles from anywhere and it'll be dark soon and we don't have anywhere to stay and YOU DON'T EVEN SPEAK SPANISH.*

But I didn't say that. In fact, I didn't say anything at all. Not a word. Like he said, he hadn't asked me to come with him. I'd practically forced him to buy me a ticket and take me to Peru. If I wasn't happy, there was only one person to blame, and that was me.

8

When I woke up in the morning, Uncle Harvey was still snoring. I went for a cold shower—the hot water didn't work—and came back and got dressed, clattering around the room, making as much noise as possible, but he didn't even stir. Eventually I just shook his shoulder and told him to wake up.

"Go away," he said.

"We've got things to do," I told him. "People to see. Treasure to find."

"I need five more minutes." He pulled the pillow over his head.

I lay down on my bed and read the guidebook. Our town wasn't even in it, so I turned to the back of the book and tried to learn some Spanish phrases.

Half an hour later, I finally managed to persuade Uncle Harvey to leave his bed. Grumbling and groaning, he got dressed and trudged downstairs to the restaurant. He ordered fried eggs and toast for both of us. "What do you want to drink?" he asked. "Coffee?"

"Ha-ha."

"You should try it. Just once. You might like it."

"I have tried it," I said. "I didn't."

"Did you have real coffee? Or that instant junk?"

"Both. I didn't like either."

"I suppose you're still very young. Wait till you're a bit older and your tastes have developed. Then you'll start to appreciate the finer things in life."

Sometimes my uncle could be very patronizing.

After breakfast, we checked out of the hotel and drove back to the shop. Uncle Harvey parked the car on the opposite side of the street and we sat there for fifteen minutes, watching people come and go, looking for any sign of Otto's men. We assessed everyone: the guy with a squawking chicken in each hand, the woman with a baby tucked into her woolen shawl, even the little old lady who could only walk with the aid of a wooden stick. Any of them *could* have been spying for Otto, but my uncle was sure they weren't. I hoped he was right.

We went into the shop, which was a junk shop in the real sense of the word. It was crammed full of old trash, as if someone had just scooped up whatever they happened to find—rusty farm implements, computer keyboards, chairs, clothes, books, postcards, old phones—and dumped all of it in here, not stopping to wonder if anyone might be interested in buying it. Sitting in the middle of all this junk was a creepy-looking man with a twirly mustache and eyebrows that met in the middle. He was reading a newspaper. When we came through the door, he gave us a long stare over the top of his paper, then said, *"Buenos días."*

"Buenos días," replied my uncle. "My name is Harvey Trelawney. I was here a week or so ago. Do you remember me?"

The man inspected Uncle Harvey for a moment, then smiled. He was missing both his front teeth and he spoke with a lisp. "You are *Inglés*? You buy the jewels? Yes?"

"That's right."

"Welcome. My name is Rodolfo, and this is my shop. Please, come, sit. You want to buy one more necklace?"

"Actually, no, I'm not interested in another necklace. I wondered if you could tell me a little more about this." Uncle Harvey opened his blue folder and took out the piece of paper. "When you sold me that necklace, it came wrapped in this piece of paper. I didn't actually look at it till I got back home. But once I did, I realized the words are English."

"Inglés? Yes?" Rodolfo was intrigued. He held the paper carefully with both hands and carried it over to the light. "Very interesting. You want more?"

"Have you got more?" asked Uncle Harvey.

"No."

"Can you get more?"

"Is possible."

"Oh, come on, Rodolfo. Let's not play games. Where did you get it? Can you remember?"

"Of course."

"So where was it?"

Rodolfo smiled. "For the necklace, you get a good price, no? How much? Two hundred dollars?"

"Seventy," said my uncle.

"Seventy. That *is* a good price."

"Oh, I see. It's like that, is it? Well, here you go." My uncle opened his wallet and pulled out a ten-dollar bill.

(Here's a piece of free advice from Uncle Harvey: Wherever in the world you might be going, it's always best to travel with American currency. In an emergency, everyone wants dollars. He had five hundred of them in his wallet. Plus a grubby stash of the local currency—soles.)

He offered the money to Rodolfo. "Will you tell us where you got it?"

"Of course. But ten dollars . . . This is not a good price."

"How much do you want?"

"Let us say . . ." Rodolfo paused for a moment. "A thousand dollars."

"A thousand! Are you crazy? I'm not asking for much, Rodolfo. Just a little tiny piece of information. Go on, take my ten dollars and tell me what I want to know."

They went back and forth like this for a few minutes and eventually agreed on twenty dollars. Rodolfo pocketed the money, handed the page back, and told us what he knew. It wasn't much. He had bought the necklace from an old man, a farmer, who came into the shop.

"What's his name?" asked my uncle. "Where does he live?"

"I show you. Come, we will go there together, you and me."

"We don't need a guide," said Uncle Harvey.

"Yes, yes. You must have guide. This place is difficult. Is dangerous. You need one guide. I will help you."

"Just draw us a map," said Uncle Harvey.

"Is not possible."

"Why not?"

"Is not possible. Come, we go now. I will guide you."

"I'll pay you for a map."

"How much?"

"How about another twenty dollars?"

"How about five hundred?"

They were going at it again, arguing over the price. Rodolfo also asked all kinds of questions, trying to discover why my uncle was so interested in the necklace and the paper, but Uncle Harvey told him nothing. Eventually Rodolfo seemed to realize that he wasn't going to get anywhere and agreed on a fee of forty more dollars. Uncle Harvey handed over the money and Rodolfo drew a map for us, showing the rough location of the old man's farm, four or five hours' drive away. Before handing over the map, he made one final attempt to join us, saying that the mountains were very dangerous and without his help we would probably spend days driving up the wrong roads, getting lost, wasting time, failing to find whatever it was that we wanted so desperately. Uncle Harvey smiled, folded up the map, and said, "Thanks for your concern, Rodolfo, but you don't have to worry about us. We'll be fine."

9

We drove for hours along tiny roads that led us out of the lush valley and up into the hills. The air grew colder, and with each bend of the road, the craggy mountaintops looked a little closer. A couple of hours from the town, we passed a patch of old brown snow, and then, soon afterward, another newer, cleaner, whiter patch. I complained about the cold, but Uncle Harvey refused to turn on the heater in the car. He said it used up too much fuel. He reluctantly agreed to stop by the side of the road so I could get a sweatshirt from my bag in the trunk.

Rodolfo's map was so vague that we weren't quite sure when—or if—we would reach our destination, but after about five hours of steady driving, we came to a rickety old house clinging to the side of the valley. It fit the description Rudolfo had given us. Geese and chickens were wandering freely through the yard, and an evil-looking mule was tethered to a post. Two scrawny dogs sprinted to meet us, snarling and growling so ferociously that I was seriously worried they were going to take a chunk out of my leg. They were followed by an old woman, bent double, leaning on a wooden stick. She shushed the dogs and blinked as if she was trying to remember where she might have seen us before.

Uncle Harvey talked to her in simple English, asking about the necklace. She shook her head, not understanding a word, and started jabbering away in her own language. He shrugged his shoulders and said, *"No entiendo, no entiendo."* They went on like this for a minute or two, and then he yanked a piece of paper and a pen from his pocket and drew a picture of a necklace. He opened his wallet and pulled out a handful of bills. Seeing the money, the old woman grinned and put up her hand, telling us to wait there, and hobbled into her house. She came back a few minutes later carrying a long silver necklace with a neat little cross on the end. It was nice enough, but not what we were looking for.

"Muchos gracias," said Uncle Harvey, handing the necklace back to the little old lady. *"Adiós."* He winked at me as if to say: *There you go — I can say a few words of the local lingo. All is not lost.*

We drove up into the hills, higher and higher.

We passed a man standing by the side of the road with a donkey and a wicker basket filled with potatoes. We showed him the picture of the necklace. He shook his head and waved us onward.

The car plunged through deep puddles and bounced over potholes, shaking us in our seats.

The air was colder. The sky was darker. The mountains towered over us.

We stopped at every farm, quizzing the owners, asking if they had sold a silver necklace to Rodolfo, the antiques dealer with the twirly 'stache.

No one spoke any English, so our conversations took ages. We had to say everything in sign language and drawings and the few words of Spanish that Uncle Harvey managed to remember.

We were offered a lot of jewelry. One farmer tried to sell us a goat. Another offered us each a glass of warm milk.

Wherever we went, I heard the word *gringo*. Uncle Harvey told me what it meant. *Gringo* is the Spanish word for a foreigner, a tourist, a white person. In other words: us.

I began to wonder if we'd made a mistake. Maybe we should have stuck with Otto. He might be a murderous criminal, but at least he could speak Spanish. Or should we have accepted Rodolfo's offer? With him in the car, guiding us, would we have found the farm hours ago? Thinking about Rodolfo, I wondered if he'd sent us on a wild-goose chase. He must have guessed we were searching for something valuable. Wouldn't he be tempted to take it for himself? He could have pocketed our money, drawn a fake map, pointed us up the wrong mountain, and waited till we were out of sight, then headed off in the right direction himself, going back to the guy who had sold him the necklace. Meanwhile we'd spend a few days driving around some completely different part of the Andes, searching for a farm that didn't even exist.

The sun sank behind the mountains. Darkness flooded the sky. Our headlights illuminated a little slice of road ahead of us and nothing more. One false move and our wheel would slip over the precipice, taking the rest of the car with it. Uncle Harvey could only drive about five miles an hour. I was tempted to get out and walk. I probably would have gotten there quicker. And I wouldn't die if the car went over the edge of the cliff.

"We're lost," I said.

"Don't be ridiculous," said Uncle Harvey. "I know exactly where we are."

"Where are we?"

He didn't answer that.

"What if we run out of gas?" I said.

"We won't."

"Are you sure?"

"Sure as eggs is eggs," said Uncle Harvey.

"What's that supposed to mean?"

"It means we're going to be fine and you should stop worrying so much."

"But I *am* worried," I said. "We can't drive all night. Where are we going to stop? Are we going to sleep out here? In the car?"

"Oh, calm down," said Uncle Harvey. "We'll find somewhere."

"How do you know?"

"Because we will. Trust me, Tom. I've been in situations like this enough times before. Something always turns up."

I didn't believe him—I thought we would have to spend the whole night sleeping in the car—but not long afterward, the road curved and our headlights gleamed over a small building. A shepherd's shack, perhaps, or an old abandoned barn. It looked uninhabited; there weren't any lights in the windows. But it had four walls and a roof, and that was enough for us.

"We'll sleep there," said Uncle Harvey. "We can carry on at dawn. I don't like driving on this road in the dark."

"Me neither."

A bumpy path led through the fields to the shack. As we shuddered and juddered up to the front door, an old couple appeared in the doorway. They must have heard our engine and seen our headlights. The building wasn't a barn. Or abandoned. Someone lived there.

We got out and talked to them.

That morning, I'd found a useful phrase in the back of the guidebook: *Teine un cuarto?* Do you have a room? I repeated it several times. The old man nodded and grinned, his teeth gleaming in the candlelight.

Uncle Harvey pulled a few bills from his wallet and offered them to the old man, who handed them to his wife.

She flicked through them, counting them quickly, then pushed open the door and welcomed us inside.

The farm had no electricity, so there was no phone, no TV, no lights, and no heating. That night was cold. There was no moon. A few candles and a flickering fire provided the only light and heat in the house. The old folks had eaten already, but they gave us some leftover boiled potatoes mixed with chopped raw onions. That doesn't sound very appetizing, I know, but it was surprisingly tasty. We couldn't speak a word of one another's languages, but we managed to communicate with a few signs and gestures, explaining we were *"Americano"* and asking if they had sold a necklace to Rodolfo. They shrugged their shoulders, not understanding what we were trying to say, and gestured for us to finish our potatoes.

I was sharing a room with Uncle Harvey. We went to bed in darkness, lighting our way with a little stub of a candle, so we couldn't see much more than the outline of the two beds that the old woman had prepared for us. Actually, they weren't really beds at all. They were just thick woolen blankets spread out on the ground, plus a couple of cushions each. I thought I'd never be able to sleep.

A voice came out of the gloom. "Night, Tom."

"Good night, Uncle Harvey."

"Don't call me that."

"Sorry. Good night, Harvey."

"Good night."

10

There were no curtains over the window, and no glass, either, so I don't know what woke me first, the sunlight or the noise of chickens cackling and scuffling in the dust outside. My hip ached. My legs, too. That's what happens when you spend the whole night sleeping on a cold stone floor.

I glanced at my uncle. He was still snoozing.

I needed to pee, but I didn't want to wake him, so I decided to stay in bed as long as I could. I lay there, mulling over the events of the last couple of days, wondering if I'd made a terrible mistake, flying halfway around the world with my uncle. I was just wondering if I'd ever see my own home again when my eyes focused and I suddenly realized what I was looking at.

I sat up and stared. Then I laughed aloud.

I threw aside the blanket, stepped across the room, and shook Uncle Harvey's shoulder.

He groaned and rolled over. "Urgh. What time is it?"

"Look at this," I said.

He reached for his watch. "Oh, it's too early. Leave me alone." And he pulled the blanket back over his head.

"You've got to look at this."

"Give me five more minutes."

"Come on. Take a look."

With a sigh, he sat up. "What's the problem?"

I pointed at the wall. "Look at the wallpaper."

"What about it?"

"Just look at it."

Uncle Harvey peered at the wall. He rubbed his eyes and stared harder. Then he threw aside his blanket too and sprang to his feet. "I don't believe it!"

"You see?"

"Ha! This is fantastic! You're a genius!"

"Thanks."

The wallpaper wasn't wallpaper at all. It was pages from a journal—from *the* journal—written in the same spidery handwriting as the page in Uncle Harvey's blue folder.

He stood on his bed and ran his hands over the wall, stroking the paper, then found a loose corner and gave it a gentle tug.

I said, "Shouldn't we ask those old folks before we tear down their wallpaper?"

"I suppose we should," said Uncle Harvey, sounding surprised, as if the thought had never occurred to him.

He pulled on his clothes and went next door. I could hear him trying to communicate with the old couple. He returned soon with a pan of boiling water. "I bought the lot," he said. "For twenty dollars." He winked at me and got to work.

11

Removing the wallpaper took most of the morning.

Uncle Harvey did it alone. He didn't trust me to help. He said I'd rip the pages. I thought he was actually much more likely to mess them up than I was, but I didn't complain. He was having a miserable time, steaming and pulling and scraping each page millimeter by millimeter. The room got hotter and hotter. His face went bright red and big pools of sweat spread across his shirt.

Some of the pages faced outward, showing their words to the world, and others had been stuck facedown to the wall. As he peeled them off, Uncle Harvey couldn't help leaving a few scraps behind, littering the plaster with tiny bits of paper and the faded impressions of old ink. We'd just have to hope those weren't the words that we needed.

The old woman summoned us for breakfast. It was a loaf of bread, two boiled eggs, and a tin of sardines, shared between the four of us and served on cracked white plates. She gave us cups of coffee, too. Uncle Harvey said his was disgusting, but he drank it anyway. I didn't touch mine.

We went back to work. The old folks popped their heads around the door to watch what we were doing. They whispered to each other. I could imagine exactly what they were saying. *These foreigners are crazy! If they've got so much money to throw around, why do they want this old wallpaper? Why don't they just go to the market and buy themselves a few nice fat goats?*

While my uncle was finishing off the wallpaper, I searched the rest of the house, hunting for any final pages that might have eluded us.

I found five.

The first was folded and wedged under a table, stopping it from wobbling.

Another was jammed in a crack in a window, keeping out a draft.

The third, fourth, and fifth were in the bathroom.

They were on a shelf just to the side of the toilet, held in place by a stone. There was a roll of grubby toilet paper there too, but I suppose they kept the pages for emergencies. The nearest shop must be miles away.

Great. That would be just our luck. There's priceless treasure buried on an island, but we can't find it because a Peruvian peasant wiped his butt with the directions.

I came out of the bathroom and ran into the old man, who was carrying a bundle of sticks in his arms. He dumped his sticks by the fire, pointed at the papers in my hands, and said something that I couldn't understand.

"Sorry," I said. "Don't speak Spanish."

He kept talking to me in the same lingo.

"I don't know what you're saying," I said. "But I guess there's not much point in telling you that, because you don't know what I'm saying either, do you?"

He grabbed ahold of my sleeve and tugged me toward the door.

I asked him what he was doing, but he just answered in Spanish. He obviously wanted me to follow him.

I thought I might as well. Why not? What was the worst that could happen?

We walked out of the house and up the field to an ancient barn.

The old man pushed the door. It creaked open. There was a rancid stench of manure. We stepped inside.

The floor of the barn was a mass of mud and straw. Junk was piled everywhere. The same family must have lived at this farm for years, and I could imagine that they had used this place to dump whatever they didn't want but couldn't bring themselves to throw away. My eyes rested on broken chairs and wooden ladders with missing rungs and various lengths of rope and an old bath and a sheep's skull and a bicycle and rusty old pipes and a piece of paper. Scrunched and scrawled with words in black ink.

I was just about to dart forward and pick it up when I noticed another. And another. And more of them; ten, twenty, fifty, trodden into the mud, buried under boxes, jumbled among everything.

The old man was grinning.

"Dollars," he said. "Dollars."

"You want more dollars?"

"*Sí, sí.* Dollars."

"No problem. You can have more dollars."

We went back to the house to find my uncle, who handed over another forty dollars, and everyone was happy.

12

I *allowed myself only a quick peek* at each of the pages as I removed them from the barn. They were all covered with the same dense black handwriting, which was pretty much impossible to read. The spelling was crazy too. A teacher would have gone through the whole thing with a red pen.

For instance: *The tayl snapt of in the myddle.*

Or: *In the nyght yt thundereth and rayneth but the after noone is fayr and hote and drye but clowdy.*

The pictures were nice, though. There was at least one on every page and sometimes two or three: a fish, a bird, a flower, a man's face. The things that you'd see on a voyage up the coast of Peru, stopping every few days to go ashore and trade with the natives or gather fresh water. They were more like doodles than serious drawings. As if the writer had knocked off a little scribble whenever he was wondering what to write next.

The final few pages were trampled into the mud or stuffed

between bricks. Up in the rafters I could see a couple of white scraps. I fetched a ladder, jammed it against the wall, climbed the rickety rungs, and pulled out a single sheet of creased old paper. I couldn't imagine how it had gotten up there.

I crept down to solid ground. Leaving the ladder propped against the wall, I walked out of the barn, unfolding the page. The sunshine blinded me for a moment, but then I noticed a funny little picture of a deer with bandy legs and two tiny horns. Next to it, in the text, my eye was drawn to an ornate capital G, the first letter of a word.

I could actually read the whole word.

It said *Golden*.

I could read the next word in the sentence too.

Hinge.

What's a golden hinge?

Would you find one on a chest filled with gold? Or a chest *made* from gold? A solid-gold chest—that would be worth a fortune!

Or did it mean something else entirely?

I read the whole sentence, trying to puzzle out the words on either side of the "golden hinge," but the handwriting was so curly and scrawled that I could distinguish only a few letters here and there. An "n" or an "m." An "o." A "t." An "ant." An "st." A capital letter that might have been an "F" or a "P."

I didn't give up. Letter by letter, I deciphered the entire

sentence. Eventually I got back to the word that had first attracted my attention. Reading it again, I realized I had misread one of the letters. It wasn't a "g." It was a "d." I had read "Hinge," but the word actually said "Hinde."

What's a hinde?

Dunno.

And what on earth is a "Golden Hinde"?

Oh.

The Golden Hinde.

Better known without that extra "e" as the *Golden Hind.*

We spent a whole year doing British history at school, so I knew the name, just as I knew the names of Walter Raleigh and William Shakespeare and Mary Queen of Scots. The problem was, apart from their names, I couldn't remember much else about any of them. If only I'd spent all those lessons listening to Mrs. McNab instead of staring out the window.

No, wait a minute. I did remember one thing. A hind is a female deer. That explained the picture. And the *Golden Hind* was a ship, captained by Sir Francis Drake.

What did I know about Drake?

I could summon up a picture of a guy with a little goatee beard.

Oh, and a fact! A useful fact! The sort of fact that would get me a big smile from Mrs. McNab. Sir Francis Drake was the first Englishman to sail around the world.

The writer of these pages might have been a sailor who accompanied Drake.

Or even Drake himself.

I piled up the pages and took them inside. Uncle Harvey was just finishing up. The room looked terrible. Plaster was peeling from the walls and the ceiling was dripping with condensation from all the boiling water, but apparently the old folks didn't mind. For sixty dollars, they would have let us rip the whole house to shreds.

I showed him what I had discovered. The drawing of the young deer and the words "Golden Hinde." And I told him my theory.

Uncle Harvey took the page from me and pored over the words. Then he looked up. "This is very interesting. You might be onto something. I have to confess, Tom, I don't know very much about Francis Drake. Do you?"

"We did him at school, but I've forgotten it all."

Uncle Harvey tapped his forehead as if he were trying to dislodge a blocked chunk of information. "Wasn't he the first man to sail around the world?"

"I don't think he was the first man," I said. "But he was the first Englishman."

"Oh, yes. After Magellan. That's right. Now I remember. Everyone calls Drake an explorer, but he was really a pirate, wasn't he? He sailed up the coast of South America, stealing gold from the Spanish."

At the same moment, we both realized what he'd said.

I could feel laughter bubbling up inside me. Uncle Harvey was grinning too. Suddenly it all made sense. We knew what we'd found and why it was here. Drake's gold. Buried on an island four hundred years ago and never seen since.

Now we just had to find it.

13

We said *"Gracias"* and *"Adiós"* to the old chap and his wife, then got into the car and drove down the bumpy track.

At a curve in the road, I looked back at the farmhouse. Our hosts were still standing in the doorway of their tumbledown home, waving to us.

I thought about the pile of papers now sitting in the trunk of the car, carefully wrapped in a plastic bag and zipped inside my uncle's suitcase. Then I thought about the old folks and their sixty dollars, and I suddenly felt ashamed of myself—and my uncle. The old couple shared their food with us, gave us somewhere to sleep, let us do what we liked to their house, waved us off, and were now intensely, embarrassingly grateful for the paltry sum of sixty dollars, which we'd handed over in exchange for the key to priceless treasure.

We hadn't actually lied to them, or even stolen from them. But it still made me feel like a crook.

I looked at my uncle, wondering if he was feeling the same way.

He was grinning to himself and whistling under his breath as he watched the road ahead. I'd never seen anyone look less guilty.

There was no point in talking to him about my doubts. He'd just laugh and tell me to stop being such a sentimental fool. Perhaps he'd be right. Instead, I asked, "Where are we going now?"

"Lima," said Uncle Harvey. "We'll stay with Alejandra."

"I thought you said we were going to stay in a hotel."

"We've got to give her car back. And she's a great cook. Plus it'll be free. Once we're there, we'll sit down with the manuscript and work out where this island actually is."

"Shouldn't we stay here in the middle of the countryside? Won't Otto be able to find us in Lima?"

"No, no. A big city is the best place to hide. Out here, we're the only gringos for miles. Whenever someone sees us, they'll know we're foreign and wonder what we're doing. In Lima, we'll blend in."

I had one more question: "Do you think it's a real island?"

"Why wouldn't it be?"

"I had a look at a map of Peru. There aren't very many islands along the coast."

"Where was this map?"

"In the guidebook."

"Didn't I tell you not to trust guidebooks? Those maps are hopeless. They only show tourist destinations. There are hundreds of tiny islands up and down the coast of Peru. Look at a proper map and you'll see them."

I wasn't sure if that made things better or worse. If there were really hundreds of tiny islands along the coast, how were we ever going to find the right one? Wouldn't it take years?

Today was Friday. We'd already been in Peru for two nights. Our flight back to New York left on Monday. Uncle Harvey could delay his and stay another week, another month, however long he wanted, but I couldn't. I had to get back to New York in time to meet Mom and Dad and pretend I hadn't been anywhere more exciting than the Natural History Museum.

"What's this?" said Uncle Harvey.

I lifted my head.

Up ahead, a big black Toyota Land Cruiser was blocking the road. Two men were standing by the open hood. They waved at us to stop. They must have broken down.

As we came closer, I got a better view of the men. They were wearing leather boots, blue jeans, and white shirts rolled up to the elbows. One of them had a pair of binoculars slung around his neck. There was something familiar about his square shoulders and his big head. Then I realized why. "It's Miguel," I blurted out.

Uncle Harvey must have recognized him at the exactly same moment, because he had already thrust his foot onto the accelerator. The car sprang forward. We headed straight at Miguel, speeding up all the time.

If someone were driving a car at me, I'd jump out of the way, but Miguel didn't even flinch. He reached under his jacket and pulled out a gun.

A gun?

A gun!

I'd seen a few guns before. My friend Benjy lives out on a farm and he has an air rifle. His dad has a shotgun. But this was the first time in my life that anyone had ever pointed a pistol at me.

I didn't like how it felt.

There was nowhere to hide. Through the windshield, I was staring at the black barrel of a gun. If Miguel pulled the trigger, it would all be over.

But before he could fire, we were upon him. The bumper was about to crack into his kneecaps. Just in time, Miguel threw himself out of our way and rolled across the road.

Uncle Harvey yanked the wheel to the left. Our little red Honda swerved and headed for the narrow gap between the Toyota and the mountainside. I shouted at him to stop—I knew we couldn't get through such a small space—but he took no notice.

I could see the other man tugging at his gun.

Where was Miguel? Why hadn't he shot us yet?

Then I was thrown forward in my seat as we crunched into the flank of their enormous car. Metal scraped against metal. The windows cracked. The engine roared. Uncle Harvey forced our car onward, ignoring its protests, jamming his foot on the floor.

I thought we'd come shuddering to a halt in a spaghetti of shredded metal, but our heroic little Honda shoved the Toy-

ota aside, both cars howling in protest, and then we burst
out the other side and accelerated down the hill, leaving a
trail of glass and paint and metal and mirrors, one of theirs
and both of ours.

Behind us there was a sound like an exploding firework.

I looked back.

Miguel was standing in the middle of the road. His right
arm was raised.

I ducked.

There were two more bangs and the car swerved.

The cliff loomed up ahead of us. The brakes screeched.
Uncle Harvey yelled and struggled with the steering wheel.
I put my hands over my face and we smashed into the hill-
side.

14

I *must have blacked out for a few seconds.*

When I next opened my eyes, Miguel was standing by the side of the car, pointing his gun at my face. He said something in Spanish. I tugged at the door and stumbled out.

Uncle Harvey was waiting for me with his hands in the air. A line of blood was trickling down his face. He asked, "Are you hurt?"

"I'm fine," I said, rubbing my head. "What happened?"

"He got the tire." Uncle Harvey nodded at the car.

I turned to look. The back tire was shredded into skinny rubber strips.

Miguel snapped an order at me and gestured with his pistol. He was speaking Spanish, so I didn't know what he was saying, but I could guess what he meant: *Shut up and put your hands in the air.* And that was exactly what I did.

There were three of them: Miguel and two other thugs,

who could have been his brothers; they had the same thick neck and broad shoulders.

Miguel kept us covered. One of the others pulled our bags out of the car and dumped them on the ground. I was waiting for him to unzip my uncle's bag and find the bundle of papers, but he didn't bother. The third thug leaned in to the driver's seat. He fiddled with the parking brake and the steering wheel. Then the two of them put their shoulders against the Honda, braced themselves, and shoved the little red car toward the edge of the precipice.

As soon as my uncle realized what they were doing, he yelled, "Hey! You can't do that!"

Miguel raised the pistol.

"No problem," said my uncle. "You can do whatever you want. I never liked that car anyway."

They wheeled the Honda to the side of the road. The front wheels bumped over the edge. They kept pushing. The little car tipped forward, nose first, and wavered for a moment as if it were deciding what to do, then slid over.

There was a series of crashes, each quieter than the one before. When the noises had stopped, Miguel motioned for us to have a look.

A couple of hundred yards below us, at the bottom of the valley, the car was lying upside down, a tangled heap of glass and metal. One of the wheels was spinning. Another had been torn off and discarded halfway down the hillside.

I thought Miguel might shoot us and toss our bodies over

the edge after the Honda. Instead he checked us for weapons, confiscated our phones, and ushered us into his own car.

We sat in the back seat with one of the thugs, who kept a watchful eye on us, cradling a pistol on his lap. Miguel sat up front with the driver. Our bags were in the trunk. And off we went.

15

It was late afternoon when we came to a high white wall and a pair of steel gates that looked strong enough to stop a tank. The driver hooted his horn. One of the gates inched open, and a man in a poncho peered warily out. When he recognized the car, he pulled back both gates, letting us in. He had a rifle slung across his shoulder and a pistol tucked into his belt. There were more guards milling around the gatehouse, equally heavily armed. This place was a fortress. Outsiders couldn't get in, and once you were inside, you'd never get out again.

We drove up a long, curving road. Neatly trimmed lawns stretched away on either side. Men in green dungarees were bent over the grass, working with rakes and spades.

Soon we arrived at a large house built around a courtyard. Whitewashed walls reflected the last of the afternoon sun. Seven black cars were parked in a line in front of the house. Through an archway, I could see the shimmering blue glare of a swimming pool.

Miguel led us into the house, down one corridor and then another. He knocked on a wooden door and waited for an answering shout, then ushered us into an enormous room with a huge fireplace at one end and a glass chandelier dangling from the ceiling. Attached to one wall there was literally the biggest TV I'd ever seen in my life. Two massive white sofas faced the screen. Otto was sprawled on one of them with a laptop on his knees. When he saw us, he snapped the computer shut and threw it on the sofa. Then he came toward us like a bull, shoulders hunched, fists raised, ready to fight. I took a step backwards. I couldn't help myself. I didn't want to be run down by him. My uncle was braver. He even managed to smile. "Hello, Otto," he said. "This is a—"

Otto grabbed his throat with both hands, his fingers digging into my uncle's neck, squeezing the air out of him.

I was about to dart forward and join the fight when something prodded me in the middle of my back. I half turned. Miguel was standing behind me, holding a pistol. I stood very still, not wanting to give him any excuse to shoot.

My uncle wriggled and writhed, trying to get out of Otto's clutches, but he wasn't strong enough. With each second, his face went a brighter shade of scarlet. His eyes bulged as if they were going to pop out of his head.

Suddenly Otto pushed him away.

Uncle Harvey doubled over, clutching his throat with both hands and gasping for breath.

"You think I don't find you?" said Otto. "In *my* country? Huh?"

"I'm very sorry," my uncle managed to say. His voice sounded scratchy and high pitched. "I tried to—"

"I don't want to hear no excuses," interrupted Otto. "Just don't do it again. Because you can't. You understand?"

"Yes."

"You too, Tom. You understand me?"

"Yes," I said.

"Good. Come here. Sit down."

We followed him to the white sofas. He sprawled on one and we sat opposite him. I looked at my uncle. He was still rubbing his neck. I could see the bruises on his skin, the red marks of Otto's fingers.

"Now, you've got one chance to make things good," said Otto. "You tell me what you find. Where's this gold, huh?"

Uncle Harvey must have decided that there was no point in lying, because he told Otto exactly what had happened to us since we left Lima. The only things that he didn't mention were Francis Drake, the *Golden Hind*, and Alejandra, simply saying that he'd borrowed the car from a friend.

Otto asked a few questions, then thought for a moment, his hands folded in his lap. We watched him in silence, waiting for his verdict. Finally he lifted his head and looked at us.

"Maybe I just kill you," he said.

"We're very close to finding the treasure," replied Uncle Harvey, smiling slightly and speaking calmly. You'd never have guessed that he was arguing for his life. "We know where it is. Well, we *almost* know where it is. We just need a little more time."

"How much time?" said Otto.

"I don't know exactly, but I should think we could do it in a day. We've got to read the manuscript and find the rest of the instructions. If we're lucky, and we work fast, we might be able to do it in a few hours."

"You can find this treasure?"

"Yes."

"You're sure?"

"I'm sure," said Uncle Harvey.

Otto thought for a moment. Then he said, "You find it, I don't kill you. OK?"

"But we had a deal," said Uncle Harvey. "We were going to—"

"You want that I kill you?"

"Of course not."

"Then shut up. OK?"

"OK," said my uncle.

"Good. Now come with me."

We followed Otto out of the room. Miguel walked behind us and a couple more guards came after him, just to remind us not to do anything stupid.

Otto took us to the library, a large room at the back of the house. There were several comfortable leather armchairs, a couple of long wooden tables, and hundreds of books crammed into shelves around all four walls.

I didn't know Otto very well, but he didn't look like much of a bookworm. Maybe having a library is a big status symbol for South American mafiosi. Even if Otto spent all his free time watching TV and playing computer games, he wanted people to think he loved curling up with a good book.

The manuscript was sitting on a table, waiting for us. There was no sign of our bags. While we were talking to Otto, someone must have gone through them, taken out the manuscript, and brought it here.

"What more you need?" asked Otto. "Food? Drink?"

"Some coffee would be nice," said Uncle Harvey. "And juice for him."

Otto spoke Spanish to one of his men, then turned back to us. "What more?"

"Nothing," said my uncle.

"Good. You need something, you tell Miguel. I come back soon, you tell me what you find. OK?"

"OK," said my uncle again.

And that was that. Otto went out, leaving us in the library with two thugs, a few thousand books, and a manuscript. We sat down at one of the tables and started reading.

Our mission was simple. The original page—the one that Uncle Harvey had been given in that junk shop, wrapped around his necklace—had ended midsentence: *We placed them at the Northern tip of the Islande in a line with th—*

We were now looking for another page that could follow on from that and tell us where to dig for treasure. I hoped Francis Drake had chosen a landmark that had survived the past five hundred years.

I pulled a page toward me and skimmed through the first few words: *We had fayr wether but scant wynd, yet I was sea-sike, I know not why. For two daies now I have ate nothing but brede and drank onlie water.*

That was a no, then.

I dumped it with the rejects and took another: *Nycolas Tindal having stoln a shirt was tyed to the maste and whipt. I begged the Captayne for mercie on his behalf but my pleas were ignored and he was beat till he bled.*

The Captayne. Who was the Captayne? Wouldn't that be Drake? If so, this journal couldn't have been written by him. The writer must be one of his crew.

Opposite me, Uncle Harvey was reading and rejecting too, although he was getting through the pages much faster. He skimmed the first sentence of the paper, checked if it fitted, then chucked it out and grabbed another sheet, not bothering to stop and worry about trivial matters like the identity of the Captayne and who might have written these words.

I knew I should be reading as fast as him. I didn't want to be killed by Otto. But I couldn't help lingering over the words. In fact, I found myself going slower and slower, reading further and further down the pages, finding out more and more about the voyage of the *Golden Hind*.

Like I already told you, I managed to daydream through an entire year of British history. But, somehow, without meaning to, I was getting interested in what I was reading.

It was the journal of a man who was sailing across an empty sea. Each day he wrote down a few facts about the weather and the ship's position. He didn't have much else to say. Maybe there isn't that much to say when your view is always the same: waves, waves, waves, and yet more waves, stretching in every direction. There were some names—Gregory Banester, John Cotton, Thomas Southern—but hardly any personal details, no interesting conversations or exciting incidents, none of the stuff that you'd get in a novel. I had to imagine it all for myself.

I found a page almost entirely taken up with a description of treasure stolen from a Spanish galleon: a chest packed with gold, another stuffed with silver, five different types of cloth, a crate of fruit, a bag of fish, a bag of bread, a bag of salt, and a barrel of "rhumm." They kept all the gold, ate the bread, and drank the rhumm.

I thought about this little ship sailing up the coast of South America, looting towns and other ships, and I suddenly understood why they would bury eight chests of gold and silver on an island. They were like thieves who broke into a house and found more money than they could carry home. Their boat didn't have enough room to fit all their loot.

I must have read fifteen or twenty pages when I found one that really intrigued me.

The writer was still aboard the ship, but now they were moored near land. He described going ashore with the captain—"our Captayne"—and catching fish in a river. Then this happened:

> As we were thus busye we chaunced to espye a greate crocodyle in the water, whom we besett with our nettes but coulde not take hym. At lengthe, after much beatinge up and downe after hym, we sett upon hym, some with calyvers, some with fyshgygges, some with speares and others with swordes. At laste Mister Doughty caste a fyshgygge in hym under the hynde legge whereat he gaped with his mouthe which was monstrous to looke upon. My couzen beinge ready with his calyver shott into his mouth. The pylot shott in his legge. Dyvers stroked hym with swordes and with pykes tille he was ded. After we kylled hym we broughte hym to the Pelican, where he was opened and flayed and my couzen, the Captayne, did order hym skinned. Tonite we dined on crocodyle. The meate was bitter and not worth the effort of findeing.

I had two thoughts immediately. The first: what on earth did "fyshgygge" mean? The second: I knew the name Pelican.

But why? Where from?

Pelican, Pelican, Pelican.

Pel-ic-an.

Pelican!

Thank you, Mrs. McNab. All those hours hadn't been in vain. When Francis Drake sailed from England, heading toward South America, his ship wasn't called the *Golden Hind*. He changed its name later, halfway round the world. No, when he left England, he was aboard a boat named the *Pelican*.

The evidence was mounting.

I read the page a second time and noticed something even more interesting than the fyshgygge or the *Pelican*.

My couzen, the Captayne.

My cousin, the captain.

I was just about to tell my uncle what I'd found when he clapped his hands together and started singing, "Fifteen men on the dead man's chest!"

"Are you feeling all right, Uncle Harvey?"

"Yo ho ho and a bottle of rum!"

"Do you want to go and lie down?"

"No, thanks, I'm good."

Miguel and the other thug were glaring at us. They probably thought we were crazy. *What's wrong with these grin-*

gos? they were saying to themselves. *What are they so cheerful about? Don't they realize Otto is going to cut them up into a hundred pieces and feed them to the piranhas?*

I said, "Have you found it?"

"I certainly have."

"Are you sure?"

"I certainly am." He picked up a sheet of crinkly parchment and waved it in the air. "Feast your eyes on this, Tommy-boy!"

16

hurried to his side of the table. He put down the paper
and stood back like a proud craftsman waiting for his work
to be inspected. This is what I read:

> small rocke which lookes likke a fishes head. If anyone
> comes after us, you must go to the angel. Look to her fifteen
> feete. Her mouth is black. She has no teethe but she has a
> deep hart and ther you will find it. When all was done and
> we were returned to the pinnace, once more our Captayne
> swore us to be secret. He sayde these monies shall lie here till
> we return. This gold and this silver, it is the property of her
> Glorious Magestie the Queene of England and none shall
> have it but her and her men.

Below this, the entries continued as normal, describing
winds and tides and dates and directions, just the ordinary
stuff of the voyage, no different from a hundred other pages
in the manuscript.

Uncle Harvey opened the blue folder, pulled out the original piece of paper, and placed it beside the one that he had just found. Together we hunched over the two sheets and read them from beginning to end.

"The dates match," said Uncle Harvey. "You see?"

He ran his finger along the numerals written on each page.

"This page goes *11th, 12th, 13th, 14th, 15th, 16th*. This one goes *17th, 18th, 19th, 20th*. The sentences match too."

He read from the bottom of one page to the top of the next:

"*We placed them at the Northern tip of the Islande in a line with the small rocke which lookes likke a fishes head*. It must be right, mustn't it?"

"I guess."

"The only thing is, what on earth does this mean?" Uncle Harvey pointed at some sentences on the second page. "*If anyone comes after us, you must go to the angel. Look to her fifteen feete. Her mouth is black. She has no teethe but she has a deep hart and ther you will find it*. It doesn't make any sense."

"Maybe it makes more sense when you're actually on the island."

"It's just so frustrating! Why doesn't he give more information?"

"He can't," I said. "He's being deliberately obscure in case this falls into the wrong hands."

"Yes, I understand that, Tom. I'm not an idiot. But he could be a bit clearer about where the island actually is."

"Maybe he did before."

"What do you mean?"

"Look what it says here." I read from the first of the two pages. *"One of them we had visited before, some days earlier, and it was named by our Captayne the Islande of Theeves for the nature of the natives.* If we can find the page where he describes their first visit to the island, then we should be able to find a bit more about its actual location."

"Let's just hope those two old farmers didn't chuck it out."

"Or wipe their butt with it."

"What?"

I explained where I had found some of the pages.

"That's just not funny," said Uncle Harvey.

At which point we both burst out laughing. The thought of that old codger sitting on the pot, realizing he'd run out of paper and reaching for the missing page of a treasure map—you either had to laugh or cry, and we laughed.

We were still giggling when the door opened and Otto marched into the library. "What's so funny?" he said.

"Just a silly joke," said Uncle Harvey.

"No problem. You tell me."

"It's too complicated to explain."

For a moment Otto considered arguing, then decided not to bother. "So, you find the treasure?"

"Not yet. But we're getting there. We've found a lot of interesting information which seems to be pointing us in the right direction."

Otto pulled back a chair and sat down at the head of the table. "Tell me."

Uncle Harvey explained what we had found and what we now needed to discover: the exact location of the island. He pulled the page toward him and read out the sentences that I had just read to him. "*We came to anchor among some islands. One of them we had visited before, some days earlier, and it was named by our Captayne the Islande of Theeves for the nature of the natives.* In other words, this was their second visit. They'd been there before. You see?"

"No," said Otto.

I took over the explanation. "We've got to put the pages in order. It shouldn't be too difficult. Some of them are dated and there are clues in others. Then we can plot their route along the coast. If we can find out exactly where they went, we'll know where they were when they found the Island of Thieves."

Otto had a lot of questions, which I answered as well as I could, keeping only a few particular pieces of information to myself. I still didn't mention Francis Drake or the *Golden Hind*. It was my first intuition, I suppose, that there might be two treasures, not just one. There was a stash of gold and silver buried on an island. Then there was this manuscript, the scribbled words of a sailor, written on only the second voyage around the world ever completed by human beings. Wouldn't that be worth something? I didn't know, but I didn't want to nudge Otto into thinking these thoughts for himself. So I simply told him that, as far as we knew, the manuscript detailed the journey of an English ship in the sixteenth or seventeenth century, sailing around the coast of South America, robbing Spanish ships and pilfering their cargoes. If we traced the voyage along a map, we should be able to discover precisely where the ship sailed and find the Island of Thieves.

Otto rubbed his hands together. "This is good work. You done well. Now you sleep. We finish searching tomorrow."

Upstairs, Uncle Harvey and I had adjoining bedrooms, each with its own bathroom.

My bag had been unpacked already, my pants and socks folded neatly away in a chest of drawers, my shirts and jacket hung in a cupboard, my toothbrush and toothpaste placed in a glass beside the sink in the bathroom. I felt as if I had been given a simple message. *There is no privacy here.*

I knew I should go straight to sleep, but I felt too wired. Too awake. Too full of thoughts. So I spent a long time padding round the room, checking out the enormous bed and the huge TV and the jacuzzi bath with its gold-plated taps, and wondering how my life would have been different if Dad were a criminal mastermind rather than a financial advisor.

17

In the morning, I pulled back the curtains and looked out of the window. I had a perfect view of the pool, its clear water sparkling in the sunshine. Otto's wife was lying in a deck chair by the diving board, smoking a cigarette.

When I left the room, I found a guard sitting in a chair by the door. He'd probably been there all night. He nodded, pulled himself to his feet, and gestured for me to follow him down the stairs.

He took me to the terrace, where Uncle Harvey was waiting. His own personal thug was there too, sitting at a chair in the shade, also smoking a cigarette.

"Good morning," said Uncle Harvey. "How excellent to see you! Come and have a spot of breakfast." He sounded very jolly for a man who didn't like getting up in the mornings. Too jolly, in fact. I realized he was telling me something. A message meant only for me. Act as if you don't have a care in the world. Whatever you do, don't say anything important. There are spies everywhere.

I nodded to the thugs and sat down opposite my uncle. "Did you sleep well?"

"I had a wonderful night, thank you. Ah! Here's Silvia."

Silvia was the maid. Somehow he'd learned her name. She giggled at his attempts to speak Spanish and filled the table with good things: freshly squeezed orange juice, a plate of pastries, and a big bowl of fruit salad. It was like being in a hotel. Apart from the thugs, of course, who watched us as we ate.

"*Huevos?*" asked the maid.

"That means eggs," explained my uncle.

"Yes, please," I said.

We both ordered scrambled. Plus toast. When Silvia had gone inside to talk to the chef, Uncle Harvey leaned back, stretched his arms toward the clear blue sky, and said, "This is the life, huh?"

"It's fabulastic," I said. "Let's ask Otto if we can stay for a month."

Uncle Harvey smiled at me. "What an excellent idea."

After breakfast the thugs escorted us back to the library. We pulled three large maps from a chest at the back of the room and spread them on one of the long tables. They fit together to form the entire coastline of Peru, stretching 1,500 miles from north to south. Then we piled up all the pages, the rejects and the ones that we hadn't even touched yet, and read through them again, searching for anything that would allow us to plot the voyage of the *Golden Hind*.

Just as before, Uncle Harvey rushed through the pages, searching for relevant information and discarding whatever wasn't useful. I found myself doing the opposite, going slower and slower, spending more and more time actually reading the words on each page, puzzling out the full story of the manuscript and its author.

All the pages were jumbled up. I wasn't reading them in any order. I'd find a page about the first days of the voyage, plowing past the coast of Spain, then reach for another and find myself in the middle of the ocean, miles from land. But I began to get a sense of the voyage, the strangeness of the experience.

For instance, I read a description of wading ashore on an unfamiliar coast and meeting natives who had never seen a European before, never seen such a big boat. They had spears and shields, but seemed friendly, until something changed—no one knew what—and suddenly they attacked, leaving one of the Englishmen dead on the ground.

On another page there was nothing except descriptions of the speed and direction of the wind. The crew must have been sailing across the Atlantic or the Pacific for day after day, driven crazy by the monotony, the endless unbroken horizon.

I was getting better at deciphering the spidery black handwriting. The spelling still stumped me, but I now knew the way that the writer did particular letters and I could skim through a page fairly easily, searching for interesting information, skipping words that didn't make sense.

Then I found something extraordinary.

It wasn't the page that I was looking for. There was no mention of gold, silver, or the Island of Thieves. But halfway down, I read this:

> *My friend Nycolas Tindal, having been syke for three daies now, cried out last nighte and then dyed. I was sitting with hym. He held my hande and asked me to take a message to his mother in Tavistok. So I shalle. He dyed like a gode Christian man and shall never be forgot. I swear this to be true and signe it now with mine owne name, John Drake. I commend his memorie to the Lord Our God.*

I read those sentences several times, making sure that I hadn't misunderstood them, and then I smiled.

John Drake.

My couzen, the Captayne.

The pieces of the puzzle clicked into place. Now I knew what I was reading and who had written it. We had found the journal of Francis Drake's cousin, John Drake. I'd never heard of him before. When we did British history, no one mentioned his name. Maybe no one even knew he existed.

I showed my uncle what I'd discovered. I could tell he was impressed, although he didn't show it, not wanting to alert our bodyguards. He said in a quiet voice, "I've never heard of John Drake. Have you?"

"No. But he was the captain's cousin. If you were going on a voyage around the world, you'd want to take people you could trust, wouldn't you? Like your cousin."

"Or your nephew."

"Exactly."

"Wait a minute," said Uncle Harvey. He pushed back his chair and walked around the walls, looking at the shelves. I waited for him, wondering what he was looking for.

He came back with a single volume of an old edition of the *Encyclopaedia Britannica*. On the side it read DELUSION TO FRENSSEN. Uncle Harvey opened the book on the table and flicked through the pages till he found the entry on Sir Francis Drake. We read it together, skipping the sections on his early life and concentrating on the voyage of the *Golden Hind*.

Midway down a page, we found this:

Contemporary accounts mention a cousin, John, born in Tavistock, the second son of Robert and Anna Drake. He was an excellent draughtsman and artist, responsible for recording the voyage in maps and drawings. These documents, along with a journal supposedly penned by John Drake, are assumed to have been presented to Queen Elizabeth when the Golden Hind returned to England. No

*trace of them has ever been found and historians suggest
that they were probably lost in the Whitehall Palace fire of
1698.*

"That's him," whispered Uncle Harvey. "That's our man."

18

We asked the thugs to summon Otto. When he arrived we showed him what we had found. We didn't tell him about the *Golden Hind* or either of the Drakes, but we didn't need to. We had enough good stuff without that. Using the journal, the encyclopedia, the maps, and our imaginations, we had pieced together the voyage of a small ship that sailed from England to the other side of the world.

"She had a crew of Englishmen," explained my uncle. "Who are, as you know, the best and bravest sailors in the world. Or were then, anyway. Most of them had been born in Devon, just like their captain. None of them knew where they were going. He refused to tell them. That was part of the deal. If they didn't like it, they didn't have to come with him. They set sail from Plymouth. I don't suppose you've ever been to Plymouth?"

Otto shook his head. "I never been to your country."

"You're welcome anytime. How about you, Tom? Been to Plymouth?"

"Don't think so."

"You should go. Your ancestors were from the West Country. It's your heritage. Anyway, here it is. The lovely town of Plymouth." Uncle Harvey plonked his finger on the map. "From here they sailed across the Channel. They went round the edge of France, over the top of Spain, and down the whole length of Portugal. Popped across the Gibraltar Straits and got to Morocco." He traced the route on the map, running his finger down the eastern edge of Europe and touching the bulk of Africa. "Not far from Essaouira, they filled their barrels with fresh water and headed south and west." Now his finger plunged across the vast emptiness of the Atlantic Ocean. "The monotony of weeks at sea was relieved only by stopping at a few islands. Here, the Canaries. And here, Cape Verde. Finally they reached your own continent. South America. They went down the coast of Brazil. Presumably you've been there?"

"Of course," said Otto. "Many times."

"They sailed down its long coast. Past Uruguay. Past Argentina. Round Cape Horn and up the other side. Up the long, long coast of Chile. And here, just into Peru, they moored at a tiny little island. The sailors traded with locals, offering knives and trinkets in exchange for fresh food and water. Midway through their negotiations, the locals made off with their booty without leaving anything in return. They were dirty thieves, said the captain, and he named the place after them."

"The Island of Thieves," I explained, in case Otto hadn't gotten the point.

He didn't take any notice of me. All his attention was focused on the map, his eyes scanning for the island's exact location.

"From there they sailed north," continued Uncle Harvey, his finger creeping slowly up the map. "They were heading for Lima. But things didn't go according to plan. They spotted another ship on the horizon. It was a Spanish galleon, so heavily laden that it couldn't sail fast enough to escape. The Englishmen captured it after a short battle. They went aboard and found that the hold was packed with silver and gold. There was too much treasure to carry on their own small ship. The weight would have sunk them as soon as they hit bad weather. The captain could have abandoned the treasure or tipped it overboard, but he couldn't bring himself to surrender so much delicious booty, so he sailed the galleon and his own ship back to the nearest island. Once they reached the Island of Thieves, the captain took a small crew of trusted men and ordered them to load eight chests onto a little boat. They rowed or sailed to the northern tip of the island and buried the eight chests, letting no one else know the secret of their location. They returned to their own ship and sailed onward. Ten days later, they were in Lima. From there they went north, past Panama and Mexico, and landed on the shores of California, not far from modern San Francisco. They turned west, cut across the Pacific, and headed for home. But that's a different story. Now let's move to the other map."

We had used two maps, one of the world and the other of

Peru. Each of them was dotted with a trail of tiny penciled crosses.

"Do you see these?" said Uncle Harvey.

Otto nodded. "That's the boat, huh?"

"Exactly. That's where it went. Each cross marks a date in the manuscript. A location mentioned by the writer. One of them is the Island of Thieves. That's where we'll find five chests packed with gold and three more with silver."

"So where is it?" asked Otto impatiently.

"Right here." Uncle Harvey put his finger on the map. "It's a tiny little place. Barely more than a speck on the map. It does have a name, though, and we wondered if you'd ever heard of it. It appears to be called . . . Isla de la Frontera."

Otto threw back his head and shouted with laughter.

We both stared at him in amazement.

"What's so funny?" I said.

"You want to know have I heard of Isla de la Frontera?"

"Well, have you?" asked Uncle Harvey.

"Of course! Everyone knows Isla de la Frontera."

"I don't," I said.

"Nor do I," added Uncle Harvey.

"You are not from Peru," said Otto. "You ask anyone in Peru, he will tell you. Isla de la Frontera, it is the most famous island in our country."

"What's it famous for?" I asked.

"It is a prison," said Otto.

"A prison," I repeated like an idiot.

"You understand what is a prison?"

"Yes. But, um, what sort of prison? For criminals?"

"Of course for criminals. What else is prison for? In truth, I spend a little time there myself. It is the place where I get this." He touched the tattoo on his neck, the snake's head. "I am there only a few months. Because of politics, you know? Here in Peru, everything is politics."

For the past few decades, Otto told us, Isla de la Frontera had housed some of the most dangerous men in Peru. The cells were stuffed with terrorists and murderers. High walls and rough seas prevented the prisoners from escaping.

He remembered a little about the security arrangements from his own months of incarceration. The guards had to stay in the prison, away from their families, and the solitude drove them a little crazy. They took out their frustrations on the prisoners and anyone who was unlucky enough to come anywhere near the island. Shoot first, ask questions later—that was their mantra.

The prison was on the east coast, facing the mainland. As far as Otto knew, the rest of the island was empty and uninhabited.

"No one never go to there," he said, his eyes gleaming with greed and excitement. "Not in a hundred years. Not in four hundred. The gold is there right now. Waiting for us. In my heart, I can feel it."

19

Later that afternoon, we flew south in Otto's little twin-propellered plane. Inside, there were three rows of wide, luxurious seats with big padded cushions. Otto sat in the first row. Then came me and my uncle. Miguel went behind us. I could imagine his eyes fixed on the back of my neck, his large hands twitching, longing to choke me to death. *Don't even try it,* I wanted to say. *Or I'll bop you on the head with another vase.*

Before we boarded the plane, I got a chance to talk to my uncle alone, and he told me not to worry, everything was going to be fine. Otto liked us, he said confidently. And trusted us. Which was why we were flying to Isla de la Frontera, rather than languishing in a cellar or staring down the barrel of a gun. I hoped he was right. I couldn't help wondering when Otto would get tired of us, or annoyed with us, and decide it was easier to kill us than keep us alive. When I said this to my uncle, he just laughed and, once again, told me not to worry.

The flight took a couple of hours. As the plane circled

before landing at a small airfield near the sea, I stared at the coastline, stretching to the horizon in both directions. Not far from the shore, I could see a couple of islands. From the plane I couldn't tell much about them. They just looked like big lumps of rock dumped in the ocean. One of them must be ours, I decided. I couldn't help grinning. We were so close! A few hours from now, we'd be setting out to sea in a little boat, making our way across the water to the Island of Thieves. I felt a sudden flutter of anticipation in my stomach. I don't know if it was fear or excitement. Probably a bit of both.

Two vehicles were parked on the airstrip; a bright red fire engine and yet another of those big black Toyota Land Cruisers. Otto must have got a discount from the dealership. Or maybe he just stole them.

A large man was standing beside the car, waiting for us. Like all Otto's drivers/bodyguards/thugs, he was wearing the familiar uniform of jeans, cowboy boots, and a leather jacket with a bulge under the left arm.

"This is Arturo," said Otto. "He is working for me down here."

Arturo nodded to me and my uncle, shook hands with Miguel, and conferred quietly with Otto. I wished I could understand Spanish. I wanted to know what was going on and what they were planning.

I still had a lot of unanswered questions. About the gold. About us. About Otto's plans. If we found the treasure together, would he give us some? Or keep it all for himself? Was he going to kill us? Or let us go? Had he already decided what to do? If not, when would he make his decision? Should we try to run away tonight? Or take our chance tomorrow? I'd whispered these questions to my uncle in the library, but he'd just shrugged and said he knew nothing more than me.

Once we were in the car, heading for Las Lomas, Otto told us what he had been told by Arturo: "The boat is ready. We can go now, but he say it is better to wait for the morning. I think he is right. We will stay in a hotel and leave one hour before dawn. That way, we are not be seen. We sail to the north. We are tourists trying for fish. We have rods and lines to make it look true. You like fishing, Harvey?"

"To be honest, I've never really seen the point."

"The point is," said Otto, "it's fun."

"I don't like killing things for fun."

"That's your problem," said Otto. He turned to me. "How about you, Tom? You like fishing?"

"Actually, I do, yeah. I've only been a few times, though. And never like this. I've only done it in a river, not at sea."

"The sea is best," said Otto. "The fish are bigger, you understand? More strong. More fighting. Maybe, after, we catch some fish. You like that?"

"Sounds good," I said.

Las Lomas was a quiet little town. Dinghies bobbed in the harbor and brightly colored fishing boats were lined along the dock. Old men sat in cafés, sheltering from the weather. The water was as gray as the sky.

"Here it is," said Otto, pointing out to sea. "Isla de la Frontera."

I could see a distant silhouette, a dark shape resting on the edge of the horizon.

There it was. The Island of Thieves.

20

On the other side of the street from the hotel, there was an Internet café. I saw it when we drove into the parking lot, and again from the window of our room. I thought about sneaking out and sending a message to the U.S. embassy or the CIA, asking for help. *We're trapped in a hotel with Otto Gonzalez,* I could say. *Why don't you come and arrest him? Or has he bribed you too?*

In the end, I didn't even get a chance to wander around the hotel on my own, let alone sneak out and use the Internet. Miguel escorted us wherever we went. He took us upstairs to our room — my uncle and I were sharing — and waited in the corridor while we showered and changed. Then he led us back downstairs again for supper.

That night there were five of us sitting around the table in the small restaurant on the ground floor of the hotel: me, my uncle, Otto, Miguel, and Arturo. A few old men made up the rest of the clientele. I don't know if they actually recognised Otto or just got the sense that he was a dangerous customer, but they were careful to sit far enough away that they had no chance of overhearing any of our conversation.

Arturo had brought a large map of Isla de la Frontera, which he unrolled and spread over the table. It was a proper nautical chart, showing the depths of the ocean and the location of navigation buoys and two lighthouses, one at each end of the island.

"This is the prison," said Otto, pointing at a structure on the eastern side. "This is the harbor. But we go here, yes?" He pointed at the northern tip of the island.

"That's right," said Uncle Harvey. He turned to me. "Tom, will you do the honors?"

"Which honors?" I said.

"Will you read out our instructions? So we know where we're going."

"Oh, yes. Sorry. Sure." I had copied the relevant sentences onto a sheet of the hotel's notepaper. Now I fished it out of my pocket and read it aloud: *"Our Captayne took the pinnace ashore and I went with him and six men also, who were sworne by God to be secret in al they saw. Here we buried five chests filled with gold and three more chests filled with silver. We placed them at the northern tip of the Islande in a line with the small rocke which lookes likke a fishes head. If anyone comes after us, you must go to the angel. Look to her fifteen feete. Her mouth is black. She has no teethe but she has a deep hart and ther you will find it."*

I'd pored over those words again and again till I almost knew them by heart, but they still filled me with a sense of foreboding and excitement. They made me imagine John Drake sitting in the cabin of the *Golden Hind*, hunched over his desk, scrawling notes, remembering where he'd just been, what he'd just seen. And they put an image in my mind: a vision of gold nuggets and silver coins spilling out of wooden crates, a fortune waiting to be found.

While I was reading, Miguel and Arturo looked thoroughly bored—which was fair enough because they couldn't understand a word I was saying—while Otto listened with an expression of intense seriousness.

"It makes no sense," he said as soon as I finished. "I can tell you, there is no angels on Isla de la Frontera. Devils, maybe. But angels? Oh, no."

"It's probably not a real angel," said my uncle.

"You trying to be funny?"

"No."

"You sure?"

"Yes. I'm just saying—"

"I know what you're saying, Harvey. I'm not an idiot. It just don't make no sense to me."

"It doesn't make much sense to me, either," said my uncle. "But I'm sure everything will become clear as soon as we get to the island."

"I hope so," said Otto.

Further discussion was prevented by the arrival of the waitress with five plates of chicken and fries.

Supper was quick and quiet. While we were eating, no one said much, and we mostly watched a big TV in the corner of the room, which was showing a soccer match. The teams were Brazilian and Argentinean, my uncle told me, and they were playing in the Copa Libertadores, the biggest tournament in South American soccer. By the end of the first half, the Brazilians were leading two to one. We didn't see the second half. After supper, my uncle pushed back his chair and stood up. "I'd like an early night," he said. "It's going to be a big day tomorrow. Sleep well, Otto. You too, guys."

"Good night," said Otto. "Sweet dreams." He gave a quick order in Spanish to Miguel, who got up too and nodded for us to follow him. In the lobby, Miguel stood aside to let us go upstairs first, then followed close behind. I wondered what he would have done if we'd tried to run away. Pulled out a gun and shot us, probably.

On the stairs, my uncle turned to me. "How did you like the guinea pig?"

"You mean the chicken?"

"That was guinea pig, Tom."

"Oh, ha, ha. Very funny."

"No joke, Tom. You've just eaten your first guinea pig. Did you like it?"

I thought back to supper. The chicken bones had seemed unusually small. At the time, I hadn't taken any notice. Just gulped it down. *That poor guinea pig*, I thought. *It should have been someone's pet, not my dinner.* Maybe it *was* someone's pet till it became my dinner.

"Don't worry about it," said my uncle, as if he could read

my thoughts. "You'd eat a bacon sandwich, wouldn't you? Or a slice of ham? Or a pork chop? Well, then. If you don't mind eating a pig, what's wrong with eating a guinea pig?"

Miguel escorted us upstairs to our room and locked us inside. *What if there's a fire?* I wanted to say. *Are we supposed to jump out the window?* I had a look, just in case, but didn't like what I saw: a long drop down to the street.

I said, "Aren't hotels supposed to have fire escapes?"

"Why are you worried about the fire escape?" replied my uncle.

"In case there's a fire."

"That's the least of our problems. What about the international criminal who wants to kill us? Or the psychopath sitting outside our door?"

"How do you know he's a psychopath?"

"I can see it in his eyes."

"See what, exactly?"

"His psychopathic tendencies."

"But what can you actually—?"

"Stop it, Tom."

"Stop what?"

"Stop being difficult. I don't want to argue about the precise definition of the word *psychopath*. We've got more important things to talk about. Come here. Sit down."

We sat on our beds, facing each other.

"I've been thinking," said my uncle. "I've decided you shouldn't come to the island. It's simply too dangerous. I'm going to tell Otto to let you stay here. We'll get you on a

bus back to Lima. When you get there, check in to a hotel
and—"

"No way," I said. "Not when we're this close."

"What if something happens to you tomorrow?"

"What if something happens to *you?*"

"That's my problem."

"And this is my problem. I don't want to get a bus to
Lima, or anywhere else. I want to go to the island. And
that's that."

"It's different, Tom."

"Why?"

"Because you're still a child. You're not old enough to
make these kind of decisions for yourself."

"Yes, I am!"

"I appreciate that this must all sound very annoying, even
patronizing, but I'm afraid it's still true. What will your parents say? Your father will kill me. I'll probably be dead already, of course, but if not, he'll definitely kill me."

"I'll tell him it's my fault."

"That's very nice of you, Tom. Particularly since it *is* really your fault. But I don't think he'll believe you. Even if he
does, he's not going to care. I'm an adult and you're a boy. I
should be more responsible. More sensible. It's my duty to
look after you and make sure you don't come to any harm.
That's what he'll say, and he'll be right. Here, I want you to
have some money." He opened his wallet and divided his
remaining cash between us, giving me a mixture of dollars and soles. "Take your passport, too. Keep it somewhere

safe. Down your pants or tucked into your back pocket. I'll give you your ticket. Tomorrow, when you get to Lima, I want you to find a hotel. Somewhere quiet. Somewhere safe. Somewhere anonymous. Can you do that?"

"I suppose so."

"Send me an e-mail," he said. "My address is very simple. Harvey dot Trelawney at gmail dot com. Can you repeat that back to me?"

I did.

"If I get your message in time, I'll come and find you. If I don't, just get on the plane and go home."

"But I don't want to—"

"Don't argue with me," said Uncle Harvey. "Not this time. There's no point. I've messed up once already. I'm not going to do it again."

21

When my uncle's alarm went off at five thirty, he slapped it with his hand and pulled a pillow over his head—whereas I sprang out of bed, full of energy, and yanked back the curtains. We might have the same last name and the same nose and even lots of the same genes, but we have a very different attitude toward mornings.

The sun hadn't risen yet. The sky was still dark. The sea was even darker. But I could see the first faint glimmers of light in the clouds. Out there, waiting for us, was the island. I was determined to get there today. Whatever Uncle Harvey might have said, he wasn't going to leave me behind. Not when I was this close.

I turned back to the lump in the bed. "Wakey-wakey," I said.

"Go away."

"Come on, Uncle Harvey. Time to get up."

"If you call me that once more, I swear I'll kill you."

"Sorry," I said. "But you really should get up."

"Give me two more minutes."

I pulled on my clothes and packed my bag, then glanced

at the clock on the bedside table. Three minutes had passed, but there was still no sign of life from my uncle. I shook his shoulder. "We have to go."

He groaned again. "One more minute," he mumbled.

"Come on, Unc— Come on, Harvey, we have to go."

"Whatever." He rolled out of bed, pushed me aside, and stomped into the bathroom. I heard him splashing water over his face and then cursing at its coldness.

When he was dressed he packed his bag, then wrapped up the manuscript in one of his shirts. He handed it to me. "That goes in your bag."

"I'm not going to get a bus. I'm not leaving you here. I'm just not."

"One of us has to get John Drake's journal back to England."

"Then you do it."

"I don't think Otto would agree to that."

"Who cares?"

"He will. And so do I. When you get back to New York, get in touch with Theo. You know who he is, don't you?"

"Your friend."

"Exactly. He's easy to find. Look him up. Professor Theo Parker at Edinburgh University. Give him a call. Tell him who you are. He'll help you authenticate the manuscript. And find a buyer. You can trust him. Tell him everything. And, um . . . tell him what happened to me."

"You'll be there too," I said. "We're going home together, remember?"

"Let's see."

I sighed, took the manuscript, and put it in my bag. I didn't know what else to do. I had hoped that he would have forgotten his whole "saving Tom" plan during the night. Or changed his mind. And, for all my determination, I couldn't actually think of any way to stay with him and go to the island.

"I'm sorry," he said.

"Forget it."

"You're cross with me, aren't you?"

"I said forget it."

I tried the door handle. Still locked. I knocked on the door. "Hello? Anyone there? Can we come out, please?"

I heard movement. Creaking. Footsteps. The key rattled in the lock, and the door swung open to reveal Arturo. He must have swapped with Miguel in the middle of the night. "Good morning," he said.

"Buenos días," I replied.

That was pretty much all we knew of each other's language.

Downstairs in the restaurant, a grumpy waitress was serving coffee and stale bread. There was nothing else to eat so I grabbed a couple of slices and a glass of cold water.

Uncle Harvey perked up after his second cup of coffee and looked around the room. "Where's Otto?"

"Don't ask me."

He waved at Arturo. "Hey, where's the boss? *Dónde está Otto?"*

Arturo jerked his thumb at the door.

After breakfast we checked out of the hotel. Someone else had already paid the bill. Arturo carried our bags to the car and put them in the trunk.

"Dónde está Otto?" asked my uncle again.

Arturo pointed toward the sea.

He drove us down to the harbor. A couple of fishermen were already aboard their boats. They gave us sly glances as they coiled their ropes.

Arturo led us along the dock to a red speedboat with a big outboard motor and a little cabin, just big enough for a couple of people to shelter from the rain. Some fishing rods and two wicker baskets were lying in the bottom of the boat. I wondered if they'd brought a packed lunch.

Miguel was fiddling with the engine. Otto was standing on the dock, waiting for us. "Good morning," he said. "Did you sleep well?"

My uncle replied for both of us. "Very well, thank you."

"Good. Now come aboard. Let's go and dig up some gold."

"Wait a minute," said my uncle. "We have to talk about something. I want Tom to stay here. He's too young for all this. Could Arturo put him on a bus to Lima?"

Otto looked at me for a moment, then shook his head. "No."

"He's just a kid, Otto. He doesn't have to be involved in all this. Let him—"

"No," repeated Otto. He said it in such a way that suggested that there was no point in arguing any further. Even so, my uncle tried to persuade him, almost begging that I should be allowed to stay behind, but Otto wouldn't budge.

So four of us boarded the boat: Otto, Miguel, my uncle, and me. *The odds aren't bad,* I thought. *Two of them and two of us. If it came to a fight, we might survive.* Sure, they had guns, but being on a boat evened things out.

Our bags stayed ashore, safely stowed in the trunk of Arturo's Toyota. I thought about the manuscript, wrapped in a shirt and zipped into my bag. Should I try to get it out and take it with me? No, that would be dumb. I didn't want to alert Otto to its value. Anyway, it was probably safer in the car than on the boat. If we managed to survive the rest of this morning, we'd just have to find some way to get it out again.

The air was bracing and cold. A strong breeze was blowing off the sea. It was a good day for sailing. If you liked danger and the taste of salt.

Further down the dock, a few weird-looking birds were squabbling over a fish. I had been watching them for a while before I realized they were pelicans. With their huge beaks they didn't look quite real, but no one else seemed at all interested in them. Pelicans were obviously just as common here as pigeons at home.

My uncle noticed what I was looking at. He said, "That's a good omen."

"Why?"

"Pelicans. The *Pelican*. Remember?"

"Oh, yes. Of course."

"Now we just need to see a deer."

"A female deer."

"Aren't they called does?"

"I don't know."

"They are. Like in the song." He hummed a few notes. "What's the difference between a doe and a hind?"

"You're asking the wrong person."

"If they hadn't nicked my phone, I could look it up on the Internet."

"Why don't you ask for it back?"

"I did. Otto said no."

Miguel started the engine. The motor throbbed. Arturo untied the boat and threw the ropes aboard. Water churned at the stern. And we were off, reversing, then turning around and heading across the channel.

As soon as we left the shelter of the harbor, the swell picked up. The wind was stronger too. Spray splashed over the front of the boat. I was wearing a coat, but I was still cold and got soaked pretty much immediately.

Up ahead, the island looked like an enormous triangle of cheese dropped into the water, tall at one end and flat at the other.

At the northern tip of the island, where we were headed, the cliffs were at their highest. Down at the south, where the island was at its lowest, we could see a few prickles of light. As we came closer, these filled out into the silhouettes of massive buildings, which looked more like factories than houses. Two hundred thieves and murderers were confined behind those walls, guarded by jumpy men with machine guns.

Miguel took us out to sea, keeping a good distance from the prison and its harbor. Now we had no protection, and the Pacific attacked us with all its force. A great cloud of spray exploded over the front of the boat and icy water dribbled down my face.

Again and again as we went through wave after wave, torrents of water came crashing down on us, soaking through our clothes, filling our shoes.

I had been sailing a few times before out of Mystic Harbor. The sea can be rough out there and I thought of myself as quite an experienced sailor, but I'd never seen anything like this.

We plunged down into troughs so deep that I thought we'd never make it up the other side. Then I'd look up and see an even bigger wave bearing down on us, tipped with frothing white spray. I would brace myself for the boat to break apart. Then we'd be tipped onto our side and swept upward.

Up, up, up we'd go, all the way onto the crest of the wave, where we would hang for a moment, balancing like an acrobat on a trapeze, the air still, the water frothing around us, and then we'd shudder and dip and plunge down, down, down into the next trough.

I kept thinking to myself: *I should be terrified. I might die. Any second now a wave will smash this little boat apart and I'll*

*be adrift, freezing, drowning, sucked under. Why aren't I terri-
fied? What's wrong with me?* I don't know the answer to that,
but I can tell you this: I wasn't scared. I was exhilarated. It
was better than any roller coaster. Imagine biking to the top
of a big hill and freewheeling down the other side, again
and again, and then speed it up, and you'll have some idea of
how good it was to be in that boat, crashing through those
beautiful waves.

Our boat did feel very small. It wouldn't take much for
a wave to turn us over and tip us out. If that happened,
we wouldn't have a chance. None of us was wearing a life
jacket, and even with them, we wouldn't survive for long out
here. Battered by the huge waves, chilled by the icy water,
we'd be dead in minutes.

I thought about John Drake, sitting in a little boat with
his cousin and six other men, pulling at the oars. Their
boat didn't even have a motor. How did they survive? Why
weren't they smashed against the cliffs?

Otto ordered Miguel aside and took command of the
boat. He steered us around the northern tip of the island
and we chugged back and forth, trying to find a landing
place.

We stood in a row, the four of us, staring at the cliffs,
wondering what we were supposed to find here.

The sun was hidden behind a thick layer of cloud, but the
sky was lighter and we could see everything now: the crags
above us and the gulls circling overhead, wondering why we
were disturbing their peace.

I searched for any sign of the landmarks mentioned in the manuscript. The rock shaped like a fish. The angel: her fifteen feet, her black mouth, her dark heart. But there was nothing. Just rock and cliff and water.

Nor was there anywhere to moor the boat. Even if we somehow managed to leap ashore, the cliffs were too high to climb. A man might be able to do it if he was brave and nimble enough, but not carrying a wooden chest packed with gold.

We fought through the waves for ten minutes, then another ten, and ten more, searching and searching, but we couldn't see what we were looking for. It was very cold. I was shivering. The others probably were too. Gradually I began to lose heart. I didn't know exactly what we had done or how we had managed to do it, but we must have misunderstood John Drake's instructions or missed a vital clue. The fish-shaped rock wasn't here.

We were in the wrong place. That was the only explanation.

I could see my uncle reaching the same conclusion. He was talking to Otto. They argued back and forth for a couple of minutes, then Otto nodded, wrenched the wheel around, and yanked the throttle down. We headed toward the open sea, leaving the island behind us.

I staggered across the cabin to my uncle. The wind howled and the waves threw me from side to side. I yelled at him: "What's happening?"

"We're going back," he answered.

"Why?"

"What else can we do?"

"Shouldn't we keep looking?"

"What do you want to look at?"

I didn't have an answer to that.

"We must have made a mistake," he said. "We'll circle the whole island, see where we went wrong. If we can't find anything, we'll go back to the hotel and look through the manuscript again." A sudden wave threw us both against the side of the boat, and he grabbed my arm. "Hey, sit down. I don't want to lose you."

I could have argued with him, but there didn't seem to be much point. What could I say? I could have asked for another ten or fifteen minutes, but what could we do that we hadn't already done? We'd looked everywhere. Searched everything. Uncle Harvey was right. We must have missed some vital piece of information. Perhaps John Drake had hidden the treasure's true location in a riddle or a puzzle and we'd actually come to the wrong island.

We could plow up and down the cliffs, battling the waves, but I couldn't imagine that we would find anything that we hadn't seen in the past half-hour.

I sat down. Miguel gave me another of his glances. I pretended I hadn't noticed and gave my full attention to the high cliffs, the circling gulls, the crags and crevices, saying a silent goodbye to the northernmost tip of the Isla de la Frontera.

And then I saw it.

I thought my eyes must be deceiving me. I blinked and stared, checking I wasn't making a mistake, but it didn't disappear. I shouted, "There!"

They turned to look at me, Miguel and Otto and my uncle, who was the only one to say anything. He called back, "What is it, Tom?"

"Look." I pointed.

"What am I supposed to be looking at?"

"That rock," I said. "The one shaped like a fish."

22

The funny thing was, none of them believed me at first. Not even my uncle. They thought I was so desperate to find the treasure that I'd just imagined a fish in a rock where none really existed. But I insisted.

"It's there," I said. "I saw it. We've got to go back."

Otto looked at me for a moment, making up his mind, then nodded and turned the boat around once more. We headed back toward the cliffs.

Uncle Harvey stood beside me. In a low voice, he said, "You'd better be right."

"I am," I said, trying to sound much more confident than I actually felt. As soon as I'd taken my eyes off the rock, the fish had vanished. Now I had moved, and the boat had too, and the fish hadn't come back again, and I wasn't even sure which was the right rock, the one shaped like a fish. Where was it? Had I imagined the whole thing? I stared at the rocks, hoping I wasn't making a fool of myself, and then I saw it again.

"There." I pointed. "You see?"

"No," said Uncle Harvey.

"There."

He followed the line of my arm, then shook his head. "I can't see it."

"There! There! Look!"

"Tom, I'm not suggesting you're making things up, but maybe your mind is playing tricks on you. When you really want something to be true, sometimes you see it or you feel it, even if it's not actually true."

"I'm not imagining anything. It's there! Look!"

"I am looking, Tom, and I can't . . . Oh, my God! You're right!" He turned to Otto. "He's right! There it is! Look!"

"Where? Where?" clamored Otto.

With Uncle Harvey's help, Otto saw it too, and his face broke into a big, gleeful grin.

Once you knew it was there, the fish's bulging eyes and open mouth were so obvious that you might have thought a sculptor had carved them out of the rock. The funny thing was, you could only see them from this particular angle. If we hadn't turned around and headed back toward the open sea, and I hadn't happened to look back at the cliffs at that particular moment, we would have returned to Las Lomas, never knowing how close we'd been, and the treasure would still be hidden in the angel's heart.

Ah, yes. The angel and her fifteen feet and her black heart. Where were they?

Staring at the cliffs, I saw her almost immediately. It was weird. My eyes must have gone over those exact crags ten times already, if not twenty, searching for features that resembled a fish or an angel, but I had seen nothing that looked like either. Now that I knew we were on the right track, I spotted her immediately. The fissures and stones shifted into a face, a body, two wings.

"That's her," I said.

"Where?" asked my uncle.

"There." I pointed. "You see?"

"No."

"Can't you see the wings? One there. The other there. And the body in between."

"I don't know what you're talking about," said my uncle. And then he laughed. "Yes! I can see her now." He slapped me on the back. "You're good at this, aren't you?"

"I do my best."

"What is it?" demanded Otto. "What can you see?"

My uncle showed him the angel.

"Ah, yes. I see her. Very good. But where do we dig?"

It was a good question.

This wasn't what I had been expecting. Ever since we arrived in Peru—no, ever since Uncle Harvey pushed the page across his kitchen table and told me to read it—I had been carrying around a picture of the Island of Thieves in my imagination. I could see exactly what it looked like. It was a small island with long sandy beaches and hundreds of lush palm trees, swaying back and forth in the brisk sea breeze. Green parrots flitted between the fronds. We would hack a path through the jungle and come to a rotting old wooden cross standing upright in the sand. In my vision of the island, I could see us, too, me and my uncle, stripped to the waist, digging down into the sand, waiting for the moment when our shovels jarred against something solid.

So what were we doing out here on the open sea? Where were the palm trees and the parrots? And, like Otto said, where were we supposed to dig?

The fierce waves buffeted us back and forth. Above us, the cliffs were grim and tall. We could see the angel, but she didn't offer us any help, any suggestions. She just lay there on the rock, blank and vast, staring out to sea.

I reached into my pocket and pulled out a damp piece of paper. The water had seeped through my jacket, making the ink run, but I could still read John Drake's instructions: *We placed them at the Northern tip of the Islande in a line with the small rocke which lookes likke a fishes head. If anyone comes after us, you must go to the angel. Look to her fifteen feete. Her mouth is black. She has no teethe but she has a deep hart and ther you will find it.*

I must have read this short paragraph a hundred times already and now I scanned it three or four times more, but it still meant nothing to me.

Look to her fifteen feete.

I could see the angel in the rock, but she didn't have one foot, let alone fifteen. Only the upper half of her body was clear; her head, torso, and wings.

Her mouth is black.

I looked above her, below her and all around her, but couldn't see anything interesting. Anything worth exploring. Anything at all, in fact, apart from solid rock sprinkled with a few sprigs of salty vegetation.

Miguel was getting impatient. He was talking to Otto in a low voice. I could imagine what he was saying. *Let's chuck the kid overboard! He's only weighing us down.* I could see Otto listening to him, deciding what to do next. He glanced at me and my uncle, then spoke quietly to Miguel. *There's no point killing these gringos yet,* he would be saying. *They might still be useful. They found the fish, didn't they? Let them find the treasure too. And then we'll toss them overboard.*

My uncle looked over my shoulder. "What are you doing?"

"Reading the instructions again."

"Found anything interesting?"

"No."

"Let me see."

I handed over the paper. The boat was swaying violently from side to side. Uncle Harvey read John Drake's words to himself. I looked up at the cliff and remembered what I had just read.

If anyone comes after us, you must go to the angel. Look to her fifteen feete.

From here, it was hard to measure distance, but I looked all around the angel, trying to guess how far fifteen feet would be.

Below her and to the left, three or four yards above the level of the raging waters, there was a black space in the rock. I hadn't noticed it before. I don't know why not. Now my eyes were drawn to the darkness, wondering what might be hidden there.

It's probably nothing, I told myself. *Just a shadow.*

Then I realized the sun wasn't shining.

23

I *stood at the side of the boat and prepared to jump.*

The waves were washing us back and forth. My legs felt unsteady. I was holding my arms out on either side of my body like a tightrope walker, trying to keep my balance. If I fell in now, I wouldn't even have time to drown or die of hypothermia; I'd just be crushed between the boat and the rocks.

Otto was standing at the wheel, struggling to put us in exactly the right position; close enough that I could leap ashore, but not so close that our hull would be smashed to pieces. On either side of me, Miguel and my uncle stood with their arms outstretched, their palms flat, ready to push us away from the cliffs if a sudden wave swept us onto the rocks.

When I'd volunteered to go ashore, I'd assumed they'd say no. I thought Otto or my uncle would insist on being the first to find the treasure. But they let me do it. I don't know why. Maybe they wanted to keep an eye on one another.

A wave swept us in. Another dragged us out. Then we

were going in again and it was my chance. I hurled myself out of the boat. For a moment so brief that I almost couldn't even feel it, I was nowhere, and then I landed on the ledge. My knees crunched against the rock. My legs flailed. My fingers scrabbled for a hold. I found a grip and pulled myself in, and I was ashore.

When I turned around, I saw that Otto had already backed the boat away, not wanting to risk the hull against these jagged rocks.

I was squatting on a narrow slab of slippery cliff. Seaweed and wild grass sprouted in the cracks. Every incoming wave crashed over me, adding another layer of water to my already soaked clothes. I was so wet through that I wouldn't have thought I could get any wetter, but I did. Water was running down my face and squelching in my shoes.

Stop complaining, I told myself. *Stop worrying. There are more important things to think about. I'm ashore. My feet might be slithering about on the rock, my hands icy, my fingers stiff and my clothes soaked through, but who cares? I'm on the Island of Thieves.*

It was time to get moving. Time to find this treasure.

I put my head back and looked up.

The cliffs towered above me, blocking out the sky. I didn't have far to go — twice my height, perhaps, or even less — but a single wrong move would send me sliding down the sheer slab of rock and plunging into the waves. On the descent, I'd probably split my skull open, and that would be the end of me.

I ran my hands over the surface of the rock. To my relief, there were lots of good holes for my fingers and ledges for my toes.

I pushed myself against the cliff and started climbing, moving slowly, stopping all the time to explore the cracks in the rock with my fingertips and the ends of my sneakers.

I was lucky. The good holds didn't run out. As I clambered higher, I found more crevices for my feet and more jagged rocks to grab with my hands. I shimmied straight up the cliff and hauled myself into the entrance of a narrow cave.

I lay on the cold rock for a few seconds, catching my breath, then stood up and peered into the gloom.

I could hardly see anything. Just the shadowy outline of some rocks, the sides of the cave, and, further in, an impenetrable darkness.

Her mouth is black.

I stepped back onto the ledge and looked down at the boat, bobbing on the waves. Three round faces stared up at me. I gave them a quick wave, then turned my back on them and walked into the cave.

It was a good height. I could stand entirely upright. I didn't even have to bend my neck.

Leaves and twigs crackled underfoot. The cave was very dry. Even in a fierce storm, the tallest waves wouldn't reach this high.

I can't imagine how they found it, but the Drakes had discovered an excellent hiding place. The narrow entrance kept all kinds of weather out of here. It kept the light out too. As soon as I stepped inside, the darkness surrounded me. I walked more tentatively now, spreading my arms, feeling my way with my fingers, waiting to touch cold rock at the back of the cave.

She has a deep hart.

My eyes gradually adjusted to the gloom. I could make out the walls of the cave, narrowing on both sides.

My foot stubbed against a heavy object.

"Ow!"

That was me speaking.

"Ow-wow-wow," my voice echoed back at me, the sound fading with every repetition.

I kneeled down and felt it with my hands, whatever it was that I'd just kicked. A block of gold? An old wooden chest? A sword? A skeleton? A skull? No. Nothing so interesting. Just a rugged chunk of cold rock.

I stepped over it and shuffled farther forward.

With each passing moment, although I was moving deeper into the darkness, I could see a little better. There were my hands, either side of me, stretching ahead, feeling their way. There were the sides of the cave, tapering inward toward a patch of intense blackness directly ahead.

She has a deep hart.

There was the floor, rough and unsteady, littered with obstacles, sticks and stones, waiting to trip me up. And there, stacked up against one wall, I could just make out a collection of shapes that looked man-made, too regular and straight to be natural. As I shuffled closer, the shapes became clearer and I realized that they looked just like boxes.

I touched the nearest.

It was a box.

Made of wood.

Old, dry wood.

Feeling my way around the sides of the boxes, pushing my fingers into the cracks and along the ridges, I counted them.

One, two. One, two. One, two. One, two.

That was the lot. A row of four, stacked two tall. Eight boxes altogether.

Here we buried five chests filled with gold and three more chests filled with silver.

Which one to open?

It didn't matter. I chose the one nearest the entrance, closest to the light. My eyes could see better now. There was neither a clasp nor a lock, just a lid fixed into the top of the chest.

I dug my fingers into the crack, trying to lift the lid. The rotten wood splintered and fell away. A splinter dug into my palm. I cursed and pulled it out. Then I tried again. This time I pushed harder, then harder still. In a sudden movement, the lid slid away, exposing the contents of the chest.

It was empty.

Oh.

I felt a great wave of disappointment.

Someone had been here before us. They'd found the eight wooden chests and looted their contents, walking away with a fortune in gold and silver. Some penniless villagers, a couple of struggling fishermen, they'd probably stumbled upon the cave by chance, searching for shelter in a storm or just mucking around when they couldn't find any fish to catch. Now they were millionaires.

Where did that leave us?

All this travel, all this effort, all for nothing.

I thought of my uncle, waiting in the boat. What would he say?

And what about Otto? What would he do? Since flying down to Las Lomas, he'd been fairly friendly. As if he liked us. How would he feel now? Would he demand his hundred thousand dollars from my uncle? Or would he just kill us right here, right now?

Wait a minute, I told myself. *Don't give up so easily. Perhaps they haven't taken everything. Someone might have sneaked in here, grabbed an armful of loot, and then bolted. They might have left a few scraps. Even a little gold or silver would be better than nothing.*

But if looters had raided these boxes, why would they put the lids back on? And stack them so neatly?

I put my hand inside the chest. And that was when I realized my mistake. It wasn't empty. It was just so dark that I hadn't seen what was inside. But I could feel it. A piece of cloth.

I gave it a little tug and felt resistance. Yes. The cloth was wrapped around something solid.

A lump.

I lifted out a heavy piece of metal about the size of an apple, wrapped in a piece of dark cloth.

I let the cloth drop to the ground, and there it was, squatting in my hand, a misshapen hunk, yellowish and glowing even in this dim light.

I'd never really understood the allure of gold. Why is this dull, soft metal worth so much? My mom has a gold wedding ring. It's nice enough, but I wouldn't say it was anything special.

This was different.

I knew that right away. By the look of it. By the weight of it. By the feel of it in the palm of my hand.

Oh, yes. This was very special. For this lump of metal, you wouldn't mind spending three years sailing around the world, enduring the cold and the damp and the danger. For this, you'd attack a Spanish galleon, dodge cannon balls, risk death.

I shuffled toward the entrance, holding the lump in my right hand, and squatted there, out of sight of the boat, not wanting to be seen by the others, letting daylight play over the surface of the gold.

I wondered how much this apple-size chunk might be worth. Thousands? Tens of thousands? Hundreds of thousands? Then I thought: *The whole crate is full of this stuff. And there are eight crates. Sure, three of them are going to be filled with silver, but that's not cheap, either. Five crates of gold and three of silver, right here with me. I'm sitting in a cave with a fortune.*

I wrapped the gold in its cloth and put it back in the crate. Then I walked out of the cave and stood on the edge of the ledge.

Otto had taken the boat farther out into the ocean, keeping the fragile fiberglass hull away from the rocks. The three of them looked up at me. Uncle Harvey shouted something. I could see his lips moving, but the crashing waves and roaring wind drowned out whatever he was saying.

I didn't even try shouting back. I just gave him a thumbs-up.

24

Otto brought the boat closer, then handed the wheel to Miguel. A strong wave forced the hull against the cliffs. A bigger bump and the fiberglass would shatter and crack open, sending our small boat to the bottom of the ocean. Miguel thrust the throttle down, taking the boat back out, then brought it slowly in again. When the boat was only two feet from the cliff, Otto sprang ashore. He was followed by Uncle Harvey, who turned and placed his boot on the boat and pushed it away. Miguel revved the engine and steered it back out to sea.

The two of them scrambled up the cliff. Uncle Harvey was wearing a rope coiled around his body. He was the first to reach me. He had a climber's body—long arms, long legs—while Otto was shorter and stockier, a fighter, not an athlete.

Uncle Harvey stood up on the ledge and peered into the cave. "In here?"

"Yes. Take it slowly. There's stuff on the floor. Don't trip over it."

He disappeared into the darkness for a few moments and emerged with a big grin on his face. "You're a genius, kiddo."

"I do my best."

He slapped me on the back, then helped Otto up onto the ledge.

Otto thanked him and stepped inside the cave. He was gone for a minute or two. When he came out, he walked straight up to me and stuck out his hand.

"This is very good, Tom," he said in his thick accent. "When we're back on the land, I buy you a drink. Many drinks."

"Thanks," I said, and shook his hand.

We got to work. Otto and Uncle Harvey dragged one of the chests out of the cave. We looked inside. Under the rotting wooden lid, the chest was stuffed with lumps of metal wrapped in old brown rags. We each grabbed one and pulled off the wrapping.

It was like Christmas. With one big difference: this year, no one got socks.

We stood there for a minute or two in a kind of daze, each of us holding a solid piece of gold in our hands, none of us saying a word. I don't know why. I suppose we couldn't quite believe that we'd actually found it. Up to now, the gold had seemed more like a dream or a story; the type of thing that would never really happen.

But here it was, in our hands, *ours*. There were all sorts of questions still to be answered. Otto had the treasure now, but was he going to keep his side of the bargain? Would he try to double-cross us? How about us? Did my uncle have a cunning plan? Were we going to try to double-cross Otto and keep the treasure for ourselves? All that could wait till we were back on the mainland. We still had work to do here.

Otto handed his lump of gold to me, then scrambled back down the cliff. My uncle and I wrapped the lumps up again, dropped them in the box, and stuffed the lid on the top, jamming it into place.

Uncle Harvey took the rope and tied one end around the chest. Then he looped the rope about a jagged corner of rock at the top of the cliff and handed the other end to me. "Hold on tight."

"Yes, sir." I wrapped the rope around my hands and braced myself against the cliff.

Uncle Harvey lowered the chest over the edge. Even though the rope was looped around a rock, the weight still yanked me along the cliff and the taut cord burned my palms, but I managed to stop it from slithering away from me.

My uncle hurried back and took hold of the rope. He looked at me. "Ready?"

"Ready."

Together, we let the rope slide slowly through our hands and lowered the wooden chest down the cliff toward Otto's outstretched arms. Every time it banged against the side of the cliff, splinters of old wood were knocked off and fell away into the water.

Once Otto had the chest safely stowed on the ledge, Uncle Harvey clambered down the cliff to join him. They untied the rope and lifted the chest between them. Then Miguel brought the boat closer to the shore. Together, my uncle and Otto heaved the wooden chest across the gap and swung it aboard the boat.

We did the same maneuver seven more times, dragging each chest out of the cave, looping the rope around its middle and lowering it down the cliff, then loading it aboard the boat. With each repetition we could do it a little bit better, knowing when we needed our strength and when we could relax.

The sixth chest got stuck on a jutting-out rock. It jammed there and tipped over. The lid slid off and a stream of silver coins spilled out, gushing down the cliff, bouncing off the rocks and spinning into the water.

Scrabbling with both hands, Otto managed to save some of them. The others splattered into the waves before my uncle and I had a chance to yank the rope, pulling the chest upward, righting it again. We held it there for a moment, waiting for Otto to stuff his pockets with silver, then kept on lowering.

That was our only disaster. Otherwise everything went well. It was exhausting work, though. By the end my arms ached and my hands were covered in red burns from the rope. Whenever I stopped for a rest, I noticed how cold I was. My clothes had been soaked on the boat. Now that I was on dry land, the chilling wind was biting into me. I could hear my mom's voice. *"Look at you, Tom! You're going to catch pneumonia."* *That would be ironic,* I thought. *Travel all the way to Peru on the trail of hidden treasure and end up with a cold.*

When the last chest had been loaded onto the boat, Uncle Harvey cupped his hands around his mouth and shouted up to me, "That's everything, isn't it?"

"That's it!" I yelled back. "All eight of them."

"Come down here! Let's get going!"

The heavily laden boat was now much lower in the water and thus a lot harder to steer. Miguel was struggling with the wheel and the throttle. Waves were already lapping over the sides, and I could see dark water sloshing around in the bottom of the boat. I hoped it would take our weight.

The boat came closer. Otto sprang aboard and said something to Miguel, who nodded and stepped aside. Otto took over the wheel. The boat was lurching on the waves, see-sawing to one side, then the other.

My uncle took a step backwards, giving himself a bit of a run-up, getting ready to leap aboard as soon as the boat came close enough. Just when he was about to jump, Miguel reached under his jacket and pulled out a gun.

I didn't have time to panic. I didn't even have time to think. I just yelled a warning to my uncle, screaming his name at the top of my voice. The wind was loud, and the waves too, but he must have heard me because he lifted his head and glimpsed Miguel. As soon as he saw the gun, he threw himself sideways.

The muzzle flashed. There was a loud bang. The gun jumped in Miguel's hand. I couldn't see where the bullet went, but Uncle Harvey hadn't been hit. He was still moving. He had his arms raised. He was shouting something. I couldn't hear what.

In the boat, Otto was standing at the wheel. He seemed to be smiling. He glanced up at me, then back at my uncle. He said something to Miguel, who took aim again.

Uncle Harvey was dodging back and forth along the cliff, doing what he could to present a more difficult target.

Miguel fired. There was a loud bang and my uncle cried out. The impact whirled him around. He doubled over, grabbing his leg with both hands, and collapsed against the cliff.

Miguel looked at Otto, who nodded.

Miguel raised his gun once more and pointed the barrel at my uncle—who was now an easy target. A wounded animal, unable to dodge or duck. Just lying there, waiting to be finished off.

I had to do something.

But what?

Yell? Scream? Try to distract Miguel?

No, that wouldn't help.

I darted into the cave, grabbed a stone, turned, and hurled it down at the boat. I was aiming for the gun, trying to knock it out of Miguel's hand, but I hit him on the shoulder instead.

At exactly that moment, he fired again. I must have knocked him off-balance, because his shot missed my uncle.

He turned to face me.

I could see his expression. He was suddenly unsure of himself. He didn't know which of us to kill first, my uncle or me. Then he lifted his arm.

First I heard the sound of the bullet hitting the rock just beside my head. Then I heard the bang. I dodged back into the cave, putting a large chunk of island between me and the gun. I heard another bang. I didn't see where that one went. Probably where I'd just been standing.

The darkness was all around me. My heart was pounding. I reached down to the ground and grabbed another rock. This one was a lot bigger. Heavier, too. I needed both hands to pick it up.

I stumbled out of the cave, lugging the rock at about knee height, and staggered on the ledge. There, I swung my arms, using the rock's weight to get some momentum.

Down below me, I could see the side of Otto's face and the top of Miguel's head and his outstretched arm, pointing the barrel of his gun at my uncle. He'd forgotten all about me. They both had. They were going to polish off my uncle first and then come for me later.

My hands opened. I didn't really aim. The rock was too heavy for that. I dropped it more than threw it.

I staggered backwards, my arms suddenly as light as air without the weight of the rock to hold them down. Almost at once I saw that I had failed. The rock tumbled through the sky and plunged straight past Miguel, missing him completely, missing Otto, too, and landing in the bottom of the boat.

I'd failed. I was dead. My uncle was dead. These thoughts were rushing through my mind when I suddenly saw Otto and Miguel throwing themselves down and scrabbling around at their feet. A great jet of water spurted out of a hole in the bottom of the boat.

Within seconds, Miguel and Otto were ankle-deep in water.

They fumbled around, first trying to block the hole, then scooping up water with their cupped hands, but the sea was too strong for them.

Otto yelled at Miguel. He must have given an order. *Abandon ship.*

Miguel tucked his gun into his belt, stepped onto the rim of the boat, and threw himself into the waves.

Otto was about to follow him, but something held him back. A rope must have wrapped itself around his shoe. Or his heel was jammed under one of the wooden chests. He bent down and tried to free himself.

By now, the boat was below the water.

I stood there, watching. I felt helpless, fascinated, repelled, horrified, all at once.

Miguel had taken a couple of strokes, swimming toward the cliff, but now he turned back again, bobbing in the big waves, checking to see if his boss was following him.

Otto must have known that he didn't have much time because he was struggling desperately, his whole body wriggling, his hands grappling with whatever had caught his foot.

He couldn't free himself.

The boat was sinking fast. He was waist deep. He grabbed the side and tried to pull himself out, but that didn't work, either.

The waves lapped at his chin.

Otto bent back his head, opened his mouth and took a last gulp of air. Then he was pulled under the water by the weight of Francis Drake's gold.

25

Miguel didn't even hesitate. As soon as he saw what had happened, he dived after his boss. The waves closed over him. White foam frothed in the place where he had just been. Then the sea burst apart and he came out again, his mouth open, gasping for breath. Once he'd filled his lungs, his body twisted, his legs kicked, and he went down again.

I stared at the water, waiting for Otto and Miguel to bob up, but nothing returned to the surface. Not a hand. Not a head. Not a boot. Not even a scrap of broken boat or discarded clothing. The relentless waves washed back and forth, giving no sign that they had just swallowed a boat, eight heavy crates, and two men.

Had I just killed two people?

I must have seen a thousand actors blown away in movies—ten thousand, maybe, if you added them all up—but none of that prepares you for witnessing the death of a real man. The funny thing was, I didn't feel sickened or appalled. If anything, I felt empty. As if the experience had wiped me clean and, just for the moment, I wasn't able to feel anything at all.

I remembered why I'd dropped the rock on their boat. Because they were trying to kill me. *And* my uncle. Looking down, I could see him lying in a heap at the base of the cliff. He didn't seem to be moving. Was he dead too?

I shouted down to him. "Uncle Harvey! Uncle Harvey!"

No answer. He didn't move.

With a sound unlike anything I'd ever heard in my life, a mixture between a scream and a shout and a gasp, a body burst out of the water.

It was Otto. He bobbed up, his face a mask of agony, and dragged a desperate breath into his lungs.

He was splashing around like a wounded animal. I don't think he even saw me. All his attention was focused on himself.

Down below me, my uncle was now moving. Sitting up. Holding his leg. I scrambled down the cliff to the ledge, then hurried along it to where he was sitting.

I said, "Are you OK? Are you hurt?"

"It's nothing. Just a scratch."

"Didn't Miguel shoot you?"

He didn't answer me. He was looking at the waves. "Is that Otto?"

I turned to look. There was Otto, making his way through the water, fighting against the powerful waves, trying to swim toward us.

"We've got to help him," said Uncle Harvey. "Give me a hand."

He kneeled on the ledge and stretched out his arm. Otto was still at least three yards away, and could hardly make any progress against the vast strength of the waves. Seeing my uncle's outstretched hand, he fought harder, his arms digging into the water, his feet kicking, but he didn't seem to be moving at all. If anything, the waves were pulling him out farther, taking him away into the depths.

He just tried to kill us, I wanted to say. *Can't we leave him in there?*

That's not very nice of me, I know, and I'm sorry, but there you go. That's what I was thinking. Why should we save the life of a man who'd tried to kill us?

Uncle Harvey yelled at me. "Come on! Help!"

I didn't argue. I just kneeled on the ledge beside my uncle and stretched out my arm toward Otto.

He might have been an excellent swimmer, but the Pacific Ocean was a lot stronger than he was. The waves flung him out, then yanked him back in again. Again and again. Toward the cliff. Then into the swell. And out again. And in again.

His strength was fading. He wasn't struggling so hard now. The waves were grinding him down.

I turned to my uncle. "I took a course."

"What do you mean? What kind of course?"

"On rescuing people from drowning. I know what to do."

What could I remember of the course? Not much. It was

just one afternoon in the Norwich town pool a couple of years ago. They taught us the basics. Mom made me do it. She wouldn't let me go sailing otherwise. That was the deal: if I did the course, I could drive to Mystic with Finn and Mr. Spencer and go out on their boat.

I yanked my jacket, my sweater, and my shirt over my head, all in a bundle. Then pulled them apart and thrust the shirt into my uncle's hands. There wasn't time to tell him how to use it. I'd just have to hope he could work it out for himself.

I pulled off my sneakers, dumped them on the ledge, and threw myself into the water. With a couple of quick strokes, I was beside Otto. I cupped my hand under his chin and pulled him back. Luckily, he understood what I was doing. People panic. I remember the instructor warning us about that. Drowners thrash about in the water. By struggling, they drown themselves *and* the person who is trying to rescue them.

My uncle had twisted one end of the shirt around his right wrist. Now he threw it out to me.

The shirt was lying on the water, waiting for me, tempting me, offering itself, promising safety.

Just out of reach.

Closer, closer.

And I grabbed it.

Uncle Harvey hauled us in. He was poised precariously on the edge of the cliff, the waves battering against him, water running down his face, and I thought, *Please don't let the water drag you in, because that would be the end of us all.*

When I was near enough to the ledge, I pushed Otto through the water toward my uncle, who dropped my shirt and reached out with both hands. The swell pulled Otto closer to the jagged cliff. Too close. Banging his head. Another surge and he was pulled away again. His hands clawed helplessly at the water.

I could see blood on his face. I grabbed him. Shoved him through the waves to my uncle again, who got him this time. Grabbing a handful of shirt. A handful of hair. Yanking him up.

Together we heaved him out of the sea and rolled him up onto the ledge, me pushing and my uncle pulling. And I rolled out too, and we lay there, all three of us, coughing seawater onto the wet rock.

26

So there we were. Stuck on a ledge. Staring at the Pacific. Nothing between us and New Zealand except a gazillion gallons of water.

Otto was breathing, but unconscious. His eyes were closed and his head turned away, but his tattoo stared up at me. The snake's eyes were fierce, its sharp teeth poised, its body coiled and ready to spring. As if it were guarding its master while he slept.

There was no sign of Miguel, but he must have been dead. He'd sacrificed himself to save his boss. Now he was five fathoms deep. Did I feel guilty about him? No. He'd tried to kill me and my uncle, and almost succeeded. If he'd been here, sitting on this rock, Uncle Harvey and I would have been dead. Simple as that. So, no, I didn't feel guilty. I just felt pleased to be alive.

And I wanted to stay this way.

Otto was coming around fast. Give him a minute or two and he'd be back to his old murderous self.

So—what next?

I pulled my coat and shoes back on. I tipped back my head and stared at the sky. I couldn't see the top of the cliff, but it was a long way up, I knew that much. I'd already seen its full height from the boat and remembered thinking: *I'm glad I don't have to climb up there.*

I looked at my uncle. He was wet through and shivering. So was I, of course, but I hadn't been shot, so my situation was that much easier. One of his pant legs was red with his own blood. He had torn a square of cloth from his shirt and wrapped it around his thigh, applying a primitive tourniquet to the wound. When I asked him how he was feeling, he said he was fine and the wound was only superficial. I hoped he was telling the truth and not just trying to be brave.

I said, "Let's start climbing."

"What?"

"Let's start climbing. Up the cliff."

He leaned back and looked upward. Then he grinned at me. "You think you could do it?"

"Of course I can. We both can."

"What will you do when you get to the top?"

"Walk across the island, find a boat, and get back to the mainland."

"It's a nice plan," said my uncle. "There's only one problem. With my leg like this, I'll never make it up there. You'll have to go on your own. Can you do that?"

"No way," I said. "We're going to escape together. Come on, this is our only option. Let's start climbing."

Uncle Harvey shook his head. "Forget about me. I'm old enough to look after myself. You'd better get moving before Otto wakes up."

Looking at my uncle, I realized I would never be able to persuade him to change his mind. He was behaving like a guy in a movie, the one who stays behind with a gun and a box of ammo, sheltering behind a rock, and blows away a bunch of baddies on his own, giving the others a chance to get away. That's fine in a movie, but no one does that in real life. Not for me, anyway. If I couldn't persuade him, I'd just have to force him. I gripped his arm with both of mine and tried to pull him up. "Come on, Uncle Harvey. Time to go."

"Didn't I tell you not to call me that?"

"You did. I'm very sorry. But can we argue about it later?"

"I'd rather argue about it now."

"Oh, just stand up!"

Reluctantly, he allowed himself to be helped to his feet. Leaning on me for support, he tested his weight on his leg.

"How is it?" I asked.

"Fine, fine."

"Not too painful?"

"No, I can't even feel it."

I wasn't sure if that was a good thing, but I didn't argue with him, just led him toward the cliff and put his hands on the rock.

"You go first," I said.

"Why me? Why not you?"

"Because if I go first, you'll probably do something stupid

like stay here. I want to see you climbing. Go on, Uncle Harvey. Get going. See you at the top."

"I hope so."

He was just about to pull himself up when there was a groan behind us. We both turned around to see Otto rolling over. He said something in Spanish and waited for us to reply. When we didn't, he mumbled, "Miguel?"

"He's dead," I said.

That woke him up. He stared at me, his eyes narrowing.

You might have thought he would say something nice to us. Like: *"I'm sorry, I didn't really mean to kill you."* Or even: *"Thanks for saving my life."* But he didn't say any of that—just, "Where are you going?"

"Up there." I pointed at the cliff.

"You're crazy," said Otto. "You'll never make it."

"We'll be fine."

He looked up at the towering cliff as if he was measuring the distance from here to the top, then back at us. "I'm gonna come too."

"No you're not," I said.

Otto just smiled. He hauled himself unsteadily to his feet. "We do it together," he said. "You help me, I help you. No problem."

He put his hands on the cliffs and searched for a good foothold.

"Tom's right," said my uncle. "You're not coming with us."

"Stop me," said Otto.

"I will."

"Yeah? How?"

"Like this."

Uncle Harvey took two unsteady steps across the ledge, swung his right arm, and punched Otto in the face.

27

Our *clothes were wet.* Our hands were freezing. My sneakers were sodden and slippery. We didn't have any special equipment—none of the stuff that climbers use: no ropes, no axes, no clips, no harnesses. Not even the right kind of boots. You have to be desperate to climb a cliff like that. And we were. Desperation drove us onward, away from the sea, away from Otto. Ledge by ledge, crevice by crevice, we hauled ourselves up the cliff, our feet jammed into the jagged shards of rock, our fingers clinging to clumps of moss.

I could have gone faster, but I didn't want to get too far ahead of my uncle. He took it very slowly, never putting too much weight on his wounded leg, and I stayed with him, ready to stretch out a hand if he needed my help.

There was a sudden screech, and a white shape flashed past me. It was a seabird, which must have been dozing on the rock and had woken up to get a nasty shock: a human face peering into her bedroom. She circled a couple of times, checking me out, then swooped down and found a safer perch farther along the cliff.

As we went higher, we disturbed more birds. At one moment a great storm of them flapped around us, shrieking and cawing, and it took all my concentration to hold on.

My arms ached. My fingers felt as if they were going to drop off. Worst of all, I couldn't stop thinking about falling. I imagined myself tipping backwards, slithering down the cliff, and landing in the ocean with a splash.

I knew I shouldn't do it, but I couldn't resist looking down.

I could see the bottom of the cliffs plunging into the fierce, bubbling cauldron of the sea. And there was a brown smudge that must have been the top of Otto's head. He was just as we'd left him, slumped against the cliff, staring at the waves.

I kept going. One step at a time. Reaching upward, searching for handholds, testing each one before using it to hold my weight and pull myself a little higher.

Farther up the cliff, I stopped once more and waited for my uncle. When he reached me, I said, "Do you need any help?"

"No," he huffed.

"Are you sure?"

"If I'm going to fall off, I want to do it alone. No point taking you with me. Keep going, Tom. Don't wait for me. I'll see you at the top."

Before starting my climb again, I granted myself another quick glimpse down at the dizzying drop, seeing how far we had come. I looked for Otto, but he seemed to have disappeared. Where was he? Had he crawled along the ledge, searching for a drier spot out of the wind? Or had he fallen back into the water?

I shifted my weight and looked down again. Then I saw him.

"I don't believe it," I whispered to myself.

Uncle Harvey heard me. "What?"

"Nothing."

"Tell me."

"He's coming after us."

Uncle Harvey nodded, as if he'd been expecting this, but didn't look down. I wished I'd been so sensible.

"Is he close?" said my uncle.

"No. But he looks as if he's moving fast."

"We'll just have to move faster."

After that, Uncle Harvey didn't waste any more breath talking. He needed all his strength to pull himself up.

I took another look at Otto and had a sudden, surprising thought. It would be very easy to drop a stone on him. Several fist-size rocks were within reach. I could grab one of them and drop it straight down onto the top of his head. He had nowhere to hide. Even if I missed the first time, I could keep going, dropping stone after stone, till I got him. And why not? He was a criminal. A drug dealer. A murderer. And he was coming after us. Why shouldn't I smash his skull open with a stone?

I wished I could have done it, but I just couldn't. Dropping a rock on Miguel had been self-defense. Dropping one on Otto would be murder.

I turned my face upward and kept climbing, trying to put everything out of my mind except hand holds and foot holds.

At last, after a long, hard climb, I pulled myself over the precipice and rolled onto the flat grass. A rest would have been nice, but I didn't have time. I crawled straight back and peered over the edge, wanting to give my uncle a hand up the last bit.

Far below me, I could see the frothing water and the waves crashing against the base of the cliff. And there was the top of Otto's head. He wasn't far behind us. Five or ten minutes from now, he'd be pulling himself up over the top too.

Here came my uncle, his fingers scrabbling for a good grip. I could see the exhaustion in his face. I offered him a hand. He shook his head. "I'm fine," he hissed. He scrambled over the ledge and collapsed beside me.

We lay there for a few moments. I listened to my uncle's breathing. He didn't sound well. I left him as long as I dared. Then helped him to his feet. We started walking. The drizzle pecked at our faces. The ground was rough, but sloping downward, and we went at a good pace.

Uncle Harvey was limping. I asked if his wound hurt. He said no. I asked if he wanted to stop and rest, and he said no to that too. I was glad. We didn't have any time to waste.

We just had to find a boat. I felt sure that if we could just get off the island before Otto caught up with us, everything would be fine.

Soon we saw the dark bulk of the prison looming out of the landscape. I couldn't see any guards. I wondered if they'd spotted us. Even if they had, we must have looked so bizarre and so brazen that I was sure they would think we were nothing to be worried about. No escaped prisoners would behave like us. Neither would crooks coming to rescue their friends in the prison. I remembered what Otto had said about the guards shooting first and asking questions later, and I hoped he was just being melodramatic.

My uncle was slowing down. I urged him onward. "We can't stop now. We can rest when we're on the boat."

He didn't answer, but he managed to walk a little faster, wincing with every step. I felt bad, forcing him along, but I knew we didn't have any choice. There was still no sign of Otto, but any minute now, he'd haul himself over the edge of the precipice and sprint across the springy grass after us.

Up ahead I could see the small harbor. A boat was tied to the dock. I could just make out three little figures unloading boxes from the back of the boat and putting them on a truck. Those must be supplies. Fruit and vegetables for the prison kitchen, perhaps.

That's perfect, I thought. *The boat will be turning back again soon. Heading home. They can take us too.*

I glanced at Uncle Harvey. If he arrived at my boat, asking for a lift, would I say yes? No way. Not a chance. He looked crazy and he had a big patch of blood on his pants. I wouldn't let him anywhere near me. But if he pulled out a handful of dollars, I might change my mind.

Once the boatmen delivered us back to the mainland, we'd buy ourselves a couple of tickets on the next bus to Lima. Today was Sunday. Our flights left tomorrow. We'd get to the airport with hours to spare. With any luck, we'd even have time to take a shower and buy some new clothes.

I was plotting the future so confidently that I didn't even notice the soldiers.

28

Six men surrounded us, shouting in Spanish. They were wearing combat pants, camouflage jackets, and polished boots. Five of them had rifles, which they were pointing at us, and the sixth had a pistol, which he kept holstered. My uncle raised his arms in the air and yelled back at them: *"Inglés! Inglés!"*

I put my hands up too. I really didn't want to get shot. Not now. Not after escaping from Otto. *We're the good guys,* I wanted to say. *We're on your side.* But I just kept quiet and tried to look harmless.

The man with the pistol seemed to be in charge. He told the others to shut up and gave us a signal which obviously meant *follow me.*

We did as we were told. Down the hill we went. Walking fast. Three guards ahead of us and three more behind.

More soldiers were waiting for us beside two khaki jeeps. One of them grabbed my uncle and shoved him toward the nearest vehicle. We clambered into the back. There weren't seats for the guards, but they clung on to the sides and we set off, bumping down a rough track toward the prison.

"Take your hands out of your pockets," hissed my uncle to me. "Slowly! Don't give them any excuse to shoot you."

I put my hands on my lap where everyone could see them.

A big pair of steel gates swung open to let us in. We drove through a no man's land of dirty earth dotted with patches of unkempt grass. Guard towers and spotlights glared down at us. Wherever I looked, I saw men with guns. Another pair of gates swung open and we were in the main courtyard, surrounded by big grim buildings with barred windows. Men were unloading crates from the back of a truck. They stopped to stare curiously at us. Then someone shouted an angry order and they returned to their work.

The jeeps parked beside a doorway. We were ordered out. We stood there for a few minutes, stamping our feet on the ground, trying to keep warm, and then one of the soldiers told us to follow him. Four of them escorted us into the prison. Along a corridor. Through a door. Then another. Down more corridors. Till we came to a little room without any windows or furniture. Two more guards were waiting for us. They stepped forward. Without a word, they started patting us down. I suppose they were searching us for weapons.

My uncle looked over at me. "How are you doing, kiddo?"

"Fine, thanks. How about you?"

"I'm desperate for a cup of coffee." He turned to the nearest guards. *"Un café, por favor?"*

The guard snapped back in Spanish.

"I don't know what you're saying," said Uncle Harvey. "I don't suppose you speak English, do you? *Inglés? Habla Inglés? Vous parlez français? Sprechen sie Deutsch?*"

This time, the guard didn't even bother answering.

They made us empty our pockets. They found our passports, the dollars and the credit cards, all sodden, but intact, and a small red penknife, which my uncle had been carrying in his back pocket.

"You can't take that," he said. "I've had it since I was ten years old."

Ignoring him, they confiscated it all.

"Oh, come on, chaps," protested Uncle Harvey. "That knife has a lot of sentimental value. If I promise not to use it, could I have it back? Please? Pretty please?"

The guards couldn't understand a word he was saying, but they probably wouldn't have cared even if they did. One of them pocketed the penknife and another took our money and passports. Then they ushered us down yet more long white corridors and through several thick steel doors.

I'd always imagined that prison guards carried big bunches of keys strapped to their belts, but this place was entirely electronic. Every door had its own keypad. I wondered how the security worked. Did they change the code every day?

Every week? Did some codes only work for some doors? I suppose I was already thinking about escaping, although the prospect wasn't exactly hopeful. Even if you found a way to sneak through the doors and past the armed guards, you'd still have to climb two fences, cross the no man's land, and get off the island.

We came to another big steel door, guarded by two more men in uniform. The door swung shut behind us, closing with a heavy clunk, and we found ourselves in a smart office with antique furniture and paintings in gold frames hanging on the walls. A thin, middle-aged man in a black suit was sitting behind a desk, typing on a computer. He had a neatly trimmed beard and small round glasses, giving him the look of a professor or a teacher. He finished whatever he was typing, then came around to meet us, speaking in Spanish.

"I don't suppose you speak French?" asked my uncle. "Or even English?"

"Of course I do," said the man in the black suit. "Which would you prefer?"

"English, please. Your accent is excellent."

"Thank you. I spent a year at Cambridge. Do you know Cambridge?"

"I know it very well. Actually, I was there myself. Which college were you in?"

"Trinity."

"Really? What a coincidence! I was there too!" My uncle was grinning as if he'd stumbled across an old friend. "Maybe we overlapped. When did you go up?"

"Oh, a very long time ago. Let me see . . . twenty-three years. And only for a year. I came to England on an exchange with Lima University."

"I'm a little younger than you," said my uncle. "We wouldn't have been there at the same time. But it's always nice to meet another Cantabrigian. Even in prison. Presumably you're not actually a prisoner here?"

The man smiled. "In a sense, yes, I am. Like the other prisoners, I cannot leave this place. But I have committed no crime. This is simply my job. I'm sorry, how rude of me. I must introduce myself. My name is Javier Velasquez, and I am the governor of this prison. My men told me that they had picked up two foreigners trespassing on the north side of the island. I hope they haven't treated you roughly."

"Not at all," said my uncle. "I have managed to cut my leg, but that was nothing to do with your men. It's not bleeding anymore, but I could do with a clean bandage. Do you think I could see a doctor?"

"Yes, of course. We have several doctors here. One of them can see you immediately. I'll take you there myself. But first, I must ask you one question. I know the English are famous for their eccentricity, but even this will not explain why the two of you are walking around Isla de la Frontera. Tell me, please, why are you here?"

"I won't lie to you," replied my uncle. "I have to admit, I was going to. I had been planning to tell you that we're tourists and we've been on a fishing trip. I would have said that our boat smashed on the rocks and we swam to shore. Perhaps you wouldn't have believed me. Perhaps you would. It doesn't matter, because I'm going to tell you exactly why we're here, Señor Velasquez. Do you know who I mean by Otto Gonzalez?"

"There is a man of that name who is famous in Peru. He is one of our most notorious criminals."

"That's him. If you're quick, you could capture him right now and lock him up in your prison."

"What are you talking about? Where is he?"

"On this island."

"How do you know?"

"There isn't time to tell you the whole story," said Uncle Harvey. "When you've captured Otto Gonzalez and put him safely in a cell, I'll tell you why he's here. For now, you simply have to catch him. And lock him up."

I could see that the governor wasn't quite sure whether to believe us. Which was fair enough. Would you believe a couple of foreigners with wet clothes who came out of nowhere and told you that a famous crook was just around the corner? But I got the sense that he'd decided to give us the benefit of the doubt. Perhaps he was persuaded by the Cambridge connection. Or maybe he simply decided it was worth taking the risk. He picked up a phone and barked some orders in Spanish. Then he put the phone down and told us that a squad of his best men would leave their quarters immediately and search the island for Otto.

"If he is here, my men will find him," said the governor confidently.

29

Two guards escorted us from the governor's office and put us in a small room. It wasn't a cell, but it wasn't exactly luxurious either. The walls were whitewashed and the tiny window had steel bars, which looked unbreakable. There was a table and four chairs. This was probably where you got to wait if you were a lawyer or a wife, paying an official visit to the prison. You hadn't actually committed a crime yourself, but you were on the side of the prisoner rather than the law, so there was no need to give you carpets, comfy chairs, or a nice view of the ocean.

The doctor was waiting for us, a black leather bag perched on his knees. He couldn't speak more than a few words of English, but he managed to communicate all he needed in smiles and sign language. He untied the tourniquet and carefully inspected my uncle's wound, then reached into his bag and pulled out a couple of bottles and a packet of gauze. He dabbed the wound with disinfectant and wrapped it in a fresh dressing.

"You lucky man," he said with a wide grin. "Very lucky man."

"It's the luck of the Trelawneys," said Uncle Harvey.

The doctor looked at him with a quizzical expression, then shrugged his shoulders and went back to work. Looking at the wound, I could see he was right. Uncle Harvey was exceedingly lucky. The bullet had gone cleanly in and out. He had lost a little blood and probably gained a scar, but nothing worse.

Uncle Harvey grinned at me. "Let's hope you've got it too."

"Got what?" I asked.

"The family luck."

"How do I get it? Just by being a Trelawney?"

"No, no. Not all of us have it. Your father doesn't, for instance. But I think you might. I still don't know you very well, Tom, but I suspect you may be a good, old-fashioned Trelawney."

"What does that mean? What's a good, old-fashioned Trelawney?"

"You don't know about our family history?"

"No."

"Nothing?"

"No."

"There's a little village in Cornwall that used to be full of Trelawneys. You should go there. Maybe we'll go together one day. Anyway, those Trelawneys were fishermen by day and smugglers by night. Some of them were hanged, others were lost at sea. A few even got sent to Australia. Those are your ancestors, Tom. Cornish pirates. I'm surprised your dad's never told you about them. Actually, no, I'm not. He probably doesn't want you to know what it means to be a real Trelawney."

The door swung open and the governor came into the room. He put our passports, money, and credit cards on the table. "Here are your documents," he said. "I'm sorry that my men confiscated them, but they are naturally suspicious of any trespassers on this island. I have faxed copies of your passports to the British and U.S. embassies. They will call me soon to confirm your identities, and then I can arrange for transport back to the mainland. I hope you're comfortable in here. Is there anything that you need?"

"Dry clothes would be wonderful," said my uncle.

"Of course. I will have some brought to you."

"And I wouldn't mind my penknife."

"Your what?"

"I had a penknife," said my uncle. "A little knife that I've owned since I was a boy. It's not worth anything, but it has a lot of sentimental value. One of your men nabbed it. Is there any chance of having it back?"

"One of my men took it, you say?"

Uncle Harvey explained how one guard had pocketed the knife while another took the money and passports. The governor looked shocked and angry. Promising to find out exactly what had happened, he hurried away.

The doctor finished his work and left us, locking the door behind him. However friendly the governor might have been, we were still prisoners.

We didn't have to wait long before a guard arrived with a bundle of clean clothes and dumped them on the floor. Once he'd gone, we sorted through the jeans, shirts, and socks, choosing what to wear. Most of the clothes fit my uncle, but they were all much too big for me, even with the shirtsleeves and the legs of the jeans rolled up. There couldn't have been anyone as small as me in the prison. I hung my own clothes over the end of a chair and hoped they'd dry soon.

"Let's call room service," said my uncle. "I'm going to have a beer and a club sandwich. What do you want?"

"A glass of water, please."

"That's all? Nothing else? Come on, Tom. We're in the best hotel on Isla de la Frontera. We might as well treat ourselves to a decent lunch. If you could order anything right now, what would you order? Steak and fries? Burger and chips? Fried chicken and chocolate cake?"

"You know, Uncle Harvey, I'm not really in the mood."

"I'm sorry," he said. For once, he didn't tell me not to call him Uncle Harvey. "Take no notice of me. I'm just being an idiot. But you can relax, Tom. Everything's going to be fine."

"How do you know?"

"Because we're safe here."

He sounded so confident that I almost believed him. "Really? What do you think is going to happen to us now?"

"With any luck, the British embassy will send someone to fetch us. Even if they don't, they'll confirm I'm British, and we'll get out of here. Velasquez won't want to keep a British and a U.S. citizen in his prison without any charge. Especially if he thinks one of them went to Cambridge. He seemed to like my story, didn't he?"

"Your *story?*" I said. "You mean, you *didn't* go to Cambridge?"

"Oh, no. I was at Edinburgh. Only for a year, actually, before they chucked me out. But I knew he'd like it if I said I went to Cambridge. Let me tell you, Tom, you should never underestimate the power of the old-boy network. There's something about those people who went to Oxford and Cambridge. If you say you went there too, they can't resist it."

I have to admit, I was shocked. I don't know why. My uncle had already confessed to me that he made a living by selling fake paintings to criminals, so what was so surprising about one more lie?

It was the ease with which he did it, I suppose. The way that he fibbed so confidently without even needing to think. It made me wonder how many other lies he might have told. To me or anyone else.

On the other hand, I was also quite impressed. Not by

his lying. Anyone can lie. But by the fact that he knew exactly which lie to tell. He was right: the governor's attitude to us had changed completely once he thought that he and my uncle had been students of the same university. Without that extra little nudge, perhaps he wouldn't have treated us so nicely. He might have thrown us in a cell and left us to fester for a couple of days while he called the British embassy and waited for them to look up Uncle Harvey's details on their computers.

"Seriously, Tom, you don't have to worry." My uncle smiled at me. "I've been in much worse situations than this. Everything's going to be fine."

"Have you been in prison before?"

"A few times."

"Really?"

"Yes. Really."

"Where?"

"Once at home. That wasn't my fault. Once in Morocco. That *was* my fault. Once in Italy. Was that my fault? Yes, I suppose so. I got caught stealing a rather fabulous statue from a palazzo in Venice. I only did it to impress a girl, and she ran away as soon as the police arrived. Never seen her since. How many times is that?"

"Three," I said.

"There must have been more than that. Let me think." He counted them on his fingers. "London, Marrakech, Venice. Oh, and once in India. That was a bit more serious.

I spent a couple of months in one of the nastiest prisons on the planet. I'd met this Australian surfer on a beach in Goa . . ."

Uncle Harvey told me a long, complicated tale about a famous supermodel, a priceless diamond, and an Indian billionaire who owned one of the biggest software businesses on the planet. I wasn't sure how much of it was true, but I didn't really care. It was a very good story.

When he finished, he said, "Your turn."

"My turn for what?"

"To tell a story."

"I don't have any stories. My life is boring. Nothing ever happens to me."

"Oh, come on, Tom. I know that's not true."

"It is, actually."

"You burned down the garden shed, didn't you?"

"I've already told you that story."

"There must be others. Haven't you ever been in trouble before?"

"Millions of times."

"So tell me what happened."

I described a few of my past misdemeanors. It was probably foolish of me, but I told him things that I'd never told anyone; I confessed to crimes that still hadn't been pinned to me. How I set off all those fire alarms at school, for instance, and the truth about Mr. Spencer's missing bicycle. In exchange, my uncle told me about his own childhood.

His wicked deeds. His appalling punishments. And what it was like having such a goody-two-shoes—my dad—for a brother.

I don't know how much time passed. A couple of hours. Maybe three or four. But we were mid-conversation, laughing about something or other, when the door suddenly swung open. We both stopped talking and looked up.

I was hoping to see a guard with a tray of food. Even better, something to drink. My throat was parched.

To my disappointment, the man who walked into our room wasn't carrying a tray or a glass of water. I was about to complain when I saw it was Arturo, one of Otto's thugs, the guy who had met us at the airfield. He reached into his leather jacket and pulled out a pistol.

We were both on our feet, ready to fight for our lives, when someone else stepped into the room and said, "I'm very sorry, Mr. Trelawney, but you have to go with this man." It was Javier Velasquez, the prison governor. He was holding two sets of stainless-steel handcuffs. "If you don't mind, I must put these on you."

"Where's Otto?" asked my uncle.

"On the mainland. This man will take you to him."

"He bribed you, did he?"

Javier Velasquez had the good grace to look embarrassed. "He is a powerful man."

"You're a prison governor! You're meant to be on our side, not his!"

"If only life were so simple." Velasquez gave us a mournful smile—as if we should feel sorry for him!—then asked us to put our hands behind our backs.

I looked at my uncle, wondering if he would try to argue, but he simply did as he was told. I could see why. Arturo had a gun; we had nothing. And we were in a cell in the middle of a heavily guarded prison.

With a clickety-clunk, clickety-clunk, the governor handcuffed my uncle's wrists, then mine. He said, "Goodbye, Mr. Trelawney. Goodbye, Tom. Again, I am very sorry. I wish things could be different. And . . . good luck."

He mumbled those last two words almost under his breath, as if he knew that they were meaningless. Our luck had run out. Then he took two quick paces to the door and called for the guards.

30

A *boat was waiting for us in the prison's harbor.* Arturo
helped us aboard. We sat in the stern and he sat opposite us,
his gun resting on his lap.

The boatman gave me a quick, curious glance, then never
looked at my face again. I knew why. If anyone asked him
any awkward questions, he wanted to be able to say, *I didn't
see anything.*

As the boat plowed through the water, heading for the
mainland, I looked at the waves and thought about jumping
overboard. Then I noticed Uncle Harvey looking at me. He
gave a little shake of his head. Somehow he knew exactly
what I'd been thinking. He was right, of course. With my
hands fastened behind my back, I'd have drowned in moments.

For the rest of the journey, I shuffled my hands around
in the cuffs, seeing if I could get some kind of purchase. In
movies, even if people are tied up, they always manage to
escape. They wriggle out of their ropes or pick the lock with

a safety pin that they happen to have in their pocket. Unfortunately, these handcuffs were tougher than that.

Once the boat docked, Arturo walked us from the dock to the hotel. We couldn't have escaped. He was right behind us, his gun in his pocket. He took us through a side entrance. A dark corridor led to the kitchens, where two women in white aprons were chopping vegetables on a wide wooden table. One of them started complaining. Then Arturo took out the gun. She laid her knife carefully on the tabletop. Arturo issued a curt order and the two women filed out, their eyes fixed to the floor.

My uncle asked a few questions — "Where's Otto? *Dónde está Otto?*" — but he didn't manage to get any response out of Arturo. Then he looked at me. "I'm very sorry, Tom."

"For what?"

"All this."

"It's not your fault."

"Yes, it is."

"It's not, Uncle Harvey. I mean, Harvey. Sorry. I don't know why I keep calling you that."

"It doesn't matter. I'm growing to like it."

"Are you?"

"No, not really. But forget it. Listen, Tom, I really am very sorry. This *is* my fault. I've behaved like an absolute idiot."

"It was my choice," I said. "I wanted to come."

"I don't just mean bringing you here. I mean even thinking I could have left you in my flat. You're just a boy. Of course you couldn't stay in my flat for a week. I should have told your dad the truth. I thought it was all a bit of a joke. Now I've messed up your whole life."

"You don't know that."

"Yes, I do."

"Come on, Uncle Harvey. We'll be fine."

He gave me a funny little smile. Kind of sad. And he said, "You're a good kid, Tom. You really are."

Something about the way that he said those words made me realize he thought we were going to die. Saying sorry was his way of saying goodbye. I wanted to say something cheerful back. To make him feel better. To make both of us feel better. But I couldn't think of anything to say that wouldn't sound amazingly idiotic. Also, I realized he was probably right.

No, there wasn't any "probably" about it. He *was* right. I saw that. Otto would come here and shoot us and that would be that.

I wish I could tell you that I faced the fact of my own death with dignity and courage, but that simply wouldn't be true. I mostly felt annoyed. I liked being alive. I didn't want to die. Not now. Not so young. Life was fun. I wanted more of it.

The door swung open and Otto entered the room. He wagged his finger at my uncle. "You people," he said. "You make me a lot of trouble, you know that?"

"You can't blame us for—" started my uncle, but Otto interrupted him immediately.

"I don't wanna hear it."

"But you have to let me—"

"Harvey Trelawney, you are one *idiota!* And not just one *idiota.* You are one *idiota* who owes me a lot of money!"

"I've already told you, I can get you a hundred thousand dollars. Just give me a couple of—"

"Forget a hundred thousand," said Otto. "Now you owe me a million!"

"A million? Why?"

"Because of that guy. The governor. He try to arrest me. Can you believe it? He try to arrest Otto Gonzalez! Lucky for him, he change his mind. But I have to pay him a *lot* of money."

"We'll pay it back," said my uncle.

"You will?"

"Of course we will."

"How you gonna do that when you're dead?"

"If you want your money," said my uncle, "you'll have to let us live."

"I've been thinking about that," said Otto. "And I decided, I've got enough money already."

Otto told us that he'd thought of leaving us in the prison for the rest of our lives. No one would ever know where we were. People might search the whole of Peru for us, but no one would ever think of looking in the prison on Isla de la

Frontera. Unluckily—or luckily, depending on your point of view—the governor said no.

"He make me promise I take you a long way away," said Otto. "He don't want you to cause any trouble for him. Even when you're dead. So I think of another plan. Is better, actually. I take you to the mountains and I drop you over the edge. With your car. You *gringos*, you always cause so much problems. Your governments, they ask questions. If you disappear, people come looking for you. This way, they will find your car, they understand what went wrong. Two *gringos*, driving in the mountains. They drive over the edge. Very sad, huh?"

"That's a good plan," said my uncle. "Can I suggest one small modification? You can kill me if you want to, but why don't you let Tom go?"

"Let him go?" Otto blinked as if he'd never heard such a crazy idea. "Why I wanna do that?"

"Because your quarrel is with me, not him. And, even more important, because he's only a child."

"What if he talks?"

"He won't."

"That's what *you* say."

"He really won't," said my uncle. "He's a good kid. He understands. He'll keep his mouth shut."

"Everyone talks," said Otto.

"He won't. Let him go, Otto. Kill me. Torture me. Do whatever you want to me. But let him go."

Otto didn't even consider it. "Is not possible. Very sorry. Now, I have to be going. Business, business, always business. Bye, guys."

He nodded to Arturo and said something in Spanish, then swiveled on his heel and marched toward the door.

"Wait!" I called after him.

Otto looked back at me, surprised. "Yeah?"

"If you kill us, you're kissing five million dollars goodbye."

"I don't need you for that," he said. "I send for divers already."

"I'm not talking about the gold. I'm talking about John Drake."

"Who?"

"The man who wrote the journal."

"I don't know what you're talking about."

"Have you heard of Sir Francis Drake?"

"You mean that old guy who goes around the world?"

"Exactly."

"I heard of him. You told me about him. So what?"

"He was John Drake's cousin," I said. "They sailed around the world together. John Drake wrote a journal of the voyage. That's what we found. That's how we discovered the location of the treasure. We've got his journal. It must be worth millions."

"He's right," said my uncle. "Francis Drake was the second man to circumnavigate the globe. A journal of his voyage is a priceless historical document. Any collector would die for it. Museums will go crazy for it. They'll be bidding millions of dollars. Tens of millions. And the best thing is, it's not even stolen. It's absolutely legitimate. The deal can be done on the open market. Kill us, Otto, and you're kissing goodbye to twenty million dollars."

"He said five million," said Otto. "Now it's twenty."

"He doesn't know anything about money," said my uncle. "Those papers are worth at least twenty million dollars and maybe much more. If you don't believe me, I can prove it to you."

"You will? How?"

"Get the manuscript and I'll show you. It's in our bags."

Otto looked at my uncle for a few long seconds, thinking about what he'd said, then muttered a quick order to Arturo.

While Arturo was gone, Otto kept his gun trained on us, making sure we didn't get any clever ideas.

After a couple of minutes, Arturo returned with our bags, one in each hand. He dumped them both on the floor.

Otto looked at our dirty, dusty bags. "You say there's twenty million dollars in here?"

"At least twenty million and maybe a lot more."

"I wanna see it."

"Of course. Let me have the manuscript."

"Where is it? In here?"

"No, in that one." Uncle Harvey nodded at my bag.

Otto reached for the bag. Then he stopped, his arm outstretched, his fingers resting on the zipper. He glanced at us, then the bag. I could see him wondering what was going on. Was this a trap? If so, what sort? What was inside the bag? Would a bomb blow the hands off whoever pulled the zip? Would a snake spring out and bury its fangs in a thief's face? A more cautious man might have left the bag behind or taken it away to open elsewhere, but Otto was too impatient, too eager. Maybe he was less interested in the manuscript than discovering what kind of trap we might have set for him; he wanted to know how clever we were. And prove that he was even cleverer. He nodded at me. "You. Open it."

"I can't," I said.

"Why not?"

"My hands are tied together. You put handcuffs on me, remember?"

Otto turned to Arturo and said a few words in Spanish.

Arturo put his gun on the table and pulled a couple of small keys from his pocket. He turned me around and unlocked one of my handcuffs, leaving the other hanging from my wrist. Then he swiveled me back and shoved me toward the bags.

I kneeled down, undid the zip, and reached inside. Otto leaned forward to watch me lifting the manuscript from the bag. Arturo must have been watching me too, because he didn't see my uncle taking two quick steps and lashing out with his right foot.

That wasn't the plan. We didn't *have* a plan. I didn't,

anyway. Or, if I did, it was simply to try and stay alive for as long as possible. But Uncle Harvey must have decided that now was the best possible moment to try something. You have to take your chances when you can, and he took his, lashing out and kicking Arturo between the legs. There was only one problem. He missed. Not completely. His foot connected with Arturo. But he didn't get him between the legs. He got his thigh instead. It must have hurt, but not enough. Arturo wasn't disabled. Just infuriated. Quick as a flash, he whirled around and punched my uncle in the face.

Uncle Harvey stumbled backwards, trying to keep his balance. Arturo leaped at him for a second attempt. Otto eagerly joined the fight. Forgotten by both of them, I darted at the table. The gun was lying there, just where Arturo had put it. I picked it up and swung around, pointing the barrel at Otto's chest.

"Hands up," I said.

I'd always wanted to say that.

Sadly, my words didn't have quite the effect that I'd been hoping for. Otto didn't put his hands in the air. Neither did Arturo. Instead, they burst out laughing. Both of them. They giggled. They chortled. They chuckled. As if I were joking. As if I were a joke. They must have guessed that I didn't have a clue what to do with a gun.

They were right, of course. But a pistol is a pistol, even if it's in the hands of a boy who doesn't really know how to use it, and I thought they really should have given me a bit more respect.

"Put your hands in the air," I said, speaking louder this time, trying to sound more confident than I felt.

Otto's smile got even wider. "You better be careful, Tom. Didn't no one ever tell you not to play with guns?"

"I'm not playing. I'm serious. Put your hands up."

"Give it to me," he said, taking a step toward me.

"Don't move! Stay there!"

"Come on, Tom. Give me that."

He took another step forward and reached for the gun.

I pulled the trigger.

The momentum jerked my arms backwards with such violence that I thought I must have broken at least one of my fingers. The bang was so loud, the whole room seemed to shake. My ears fizzed.

For a moment, Otto carried on smiling. Then he realized that there was a man on the ground behind him, screaming and spilling scarlet blood all over the nice clean floor.

Look, I never wanted to shoot anyone. But it was a choice between them and me. If I didn't pull the trigger, they would have taken the pistol out of my hands and blown my head off. So I shot him in the leg.

Sorry, Arturo.

I could see Otto calculating his next move. He didn't want to be shot. He knew I might go for the head or the heart this time.

I don't know if I would have. Or could have. Even if I had, I probably would have missed. Luckily I didn't have to make the choice. Otto backed away and put his hands in the air. "No problem, Tom. Let's keep calm, huh?"

"I'm very calm," I said.

"Good. So let's talk. What you want? Money?"

"No. I want to get out of here."

"You wanna car? Or a plane? How 'bout that, Tom? You wanna borrow my plane?"

"Give us the keys," said my uncle.

"What keys?" asked Otto.

"The keys to your car."

"I don't have no keys."

"Then where are they?"

"I don't know. Anyway, forget the keys. You don't need no car. You can have my plane. How 'bout that? Don't you want my plane?"

I realized what he was doing. The hotel was probably full of his men, who must have heard the shot. They'd come running. If Otto could keep us talking for a minute or two, we'd be outnumbered.

I swung the gun at the wall just above his head and pulled the trigger. This time, the bang was even louder. My ears were ringing.

I turned the gun on Otto.

"Give me the keys," I said.

"No problem. Here you go." He stepped toward me, pulling a bunch of keys from his pocket.

"Stay there!"

He stopped. I saw his eyes skittering around the room, resting for an instant on Uncle Harvey, then on Arturo, who was still in a heap on the floor, clutching his leg, trying to stop the flow of blood. Otto's eyes came back to me and I could see him measuring his chances, wondering what would happen if he jumped at me.

"Put the keys on the ground," I said. "Push them over here."

Very slowly, he kneeled down and scooted the keys across the floor toward me.

They were at my feet. I didn't pick them up.

"Turn around," I said.

"You gonna shoot me?" said Otto.

"No."

"You better not."

"I said I won't."

"Let me tell you, Tom, if you —"

"Turn around!"

He looked at me for a long moment. What could he do? Run away? Fight me? Try to make a deal? Finally he accepted that he didn't have any choice. He turned and faced the wall.

31

Did Otto really think I'd shoot him in the back of the head?

Of course he did. Because if he'd been me, that was exactly what he would have done. Bang! Bang! Two bullets to the brain. All problems solved. But murdering people really wasn't my style. I grabbed the keys from the floor and headed for the door. Then I remembered the manuscript. I darted back, scooped it up, and ran after Uncle Harvey, who was already sprinting out of the kitchen.

I followed him down the corridor and through the door. In the yard, Uncle Harvey was standing beside the Toyota. He yelled: "Unlock it!"

"There's no time," I shouted back. "Let's just run."

"Why do we need to run? We've got a car."

"You can't drive. Your hands are tied together."

"*You're* going to drive."

"*Me?*"

"Stop making that stupid face, Tom, and open the doors!"

"Arturo's got the keys to your handcuffs," I said. "Why don't I run back in there and—"

"Open the doors!" yelled Uncle Harvey.

I went through the keys, looking for the right one. My head felt light and airy. As if I'd been holding my breath for a long time. My hands were shaking and my fingers still hurt. I said, "I don't know which one it is."

"Come here."

I ran to my uncle. He nodded at the keys. "That one. No, that one! Yes. Point it at the car and press that button."

I did as I was told. The indicator lights flashed twice. I opened the door and helped my uncle inside. I could hear shouts coming from the hotel. I looked up. In one of the second-floor windows, I saw the shape of a man. He was trying to open the catch. As I watched him, he gave up the struggle and smashed the glass with the butt of his pistol. Then he leaned out and pointed a gun at me.

I ran around the front of the car.

There was a bang. Gravel spurted near my feet. I yanked the door open.

Another bang. I didn't see where that bullet went. I swung the manuscript inside and hurled myself after it, landing in a heap on the driver's seat.

The Toyota was designed for someone bigger than me, but with a bit of stretching, I managed to put my hands and feet in the right places. I could even see where I was going. Just.

I'd never actually driven a car before. I'd often asked Dad to teach me. He always said no. Told me to wait till I was seventeen. But I'd been driven a million times by him and Mom, and I'd carefully watched what they did, preparing myself for the moment that I could have a go. Luckily the Toyota was an automatic, just like theirs, so I knew exactly what to do. I slid the keys into the ignition, turned on the engine, put the gearstick into drive and rammed my foot on the accelerator. The car juddered and whined like a dog straining at the leash.

"The brake!" yelled Uncle Harvey.

Oh, yes. Good point. I'd forgotten that.

Once I took off the emergency brake and pushed my toe on the accelerator again, the Toyota sprang across the court-yard and, with a mighty crash, drove straight into the side of a white van. Glass tinkled. Metal squealed. I thrust my foot deeper onto the accelerator and hauled the wheel to the left. I caught a quick glimpse of the van, its flank dented, its window smashed, and then we were rushing toward the exit.

Somewhere in the distance, I heard another bang, but I didn't have time to worry about bullets now. If one hit me, I'd know about it soon enough. With an agonizing squeal of metal scraping against brick, we shuddered against the gate post, losing one of our side mirrors. Then we were on the road.

Right ahead of me, I saw a man with a rolled-up newspaper tucked under his arm, sauntering along the street. He stopped. Stared at us. Opened his mouth to scream. And, just in time, remembered to throw himself out of our way.

"How're you doing?" shouted Uncle Harvey.

"Good, thanks."

And I was. Considering this was my first time driving a car, I thought things were going quite well. No one had been hurt and the Toyota was moving faster all the time. Then I saw Otto.

He was standing in the middle of the road. I don't know how he got there so fast, or where he found a gun, but he was prepared for us. Ready and waiting. His hands were raised. He was pointing the pistol directly at me. I could see its small black eye. Which was suddenly obscured by a red flash.

Right in front of me, a hole appeared in the glass. I felt something brush my cheek. As gentle as a finger.

There wasn't time to think. I couldn't make a decision, let alone consult with my uncle. I just carried on doing what I was doing and headed straight for Otto.

Another bang. Another red flash. Cracks splintered the windshield. Cold air rushed over my face and the car was full of noise.

A third shot would have killed me, but Otto didn't have time to pull the trigger again before the front of the car rammed into him. There was a thud. And a loud scream. Then we were past him and roaring down the main street.

My uncle shifted in his seat, looking back, but I kept facing forward, my hands on the wheel, my foot on the accelerator. A kid on a bike swerved, fell off, and rolled across the road, missing us by a millimeter. I drove past women with shopping bags, and a man in a white apron, and a waitress with a tray of glasses, all of them stopping and staring, their faces carved open by astonishment. Then they were behind us. Soon the town was too. We were careening along the coast road, palm trees on one side and the sea on the other.

"Should I stop?" I yelled.

"Not yet."

"When?"

"Soon. Just keep doing what you're doing. It's perfect."

I drove for about ten minutes without hitting anything. Then Uncle Harvey said, "You see that gas station?"

"Yes."

"That's where we'll stop."

"Fine," I said. And then: "How do I do that?"

"How do you do what?"

"How do I stop?"

"Lift your foot gently off the accelerator and apply it smoothly but firmly to the brake."

I tried to do exactly what he told me, but I couldn't have got it quite right, because the car swerved, skidded, and smashed into a tree. A shower of leaves fluttered down onto the windshield. A mechanic came running out of the garage and stood in front, staring at us and wiping his oily hands on his blue overalls.

"Perfect," said Uncle Harvey. "Where did you learn to drive like that?"

"Actually, it was my first time."

"I'd never have guessed. Now let's ask this nice man if he can lend us a chisel."

32

Uncle Harvey was a much better driver than I was. We roared up the road away from the garage, leaving the mechanic in a cloud of dust. In exchange for a damp fifty-dollar bill, he'd happily hammered the handcuffs from our wrists.

I glanced at the speedometer. The needle was on 150 and still climbing. That was kilometers per hour, not miles, but even so, we were moving exceedingly fast. The headlights were smashed, the side mirrors had gone, and the windshield was peppered with bullet holes, but that big black Toyota still went like a rocket.

Stopping only to buy a couple of delicious chicken sandwiches from a wooden shack by the side of the road, we got to Lima twice as fast as any bus. We bypassed the city itself and found a cheap hotel near the airport. The clerk at the desk said we couldn't have a room unless we showed our passports, but she changed her mind when Uncle Harvey offered to pay double.

Why didn't we want to show our passports? In case the

clerk was one of Otto's spies, reporting back to him on the movements of two suspicious-looking gringos. He might have been dead, of course, but Otto Gonzalez looked like a survivor, and I wouldn't have been surprised if he'd picked himself up, dusted himself off, grabbed a phone, and called all his pals up and down the country, promising an enormous reward for our capture, dead or alive.

We sauntered out of the hotel, telling the clerk that we'd be back for dinner. Then we took a taxi straight to the airport, where Uncle Harvey bought a couple of tickets on the next flight to Miami. They cost almost four thousand dollars. For five thousand more, he got us both on a connecting flight from Miami to New York. His credit card didn't even flinch.

Two planes, a train, a taxi, and twenty-one hours later, we climbed the steps to Uncle Harvey's apartment. My parents were due any second. I looked up and down the street, but I couldn't see the family wagon. Maybe their flight had been delayed.

Uncle Harvey's keys were still in his bag, which might have been anywhere by now, so he rang a neighbor's bell and borrowed his spare set from her. She was a little old lady with white hair and bright pink spectacles. As she handed over his keys, she said, "It's a lovely morning, isn't it?"

"Beautiful," said Uncle Harvey.

And it was. The sun was shining. The birds were singing in the trees. All was well with the world.

We went upstairs. I had a shower and changed into some clean clothes that my uncle had unearthed for me: a pair of jeans and a T-shirt that had belonged to one of his ex-girlfriends. To my surprise, they fit almost perfectly. He shaved and showered too, then put the kettle on, and it had just boiled when the doorbell rang.

"You want to get it?" he said. "Or shall I?"

"I'll go."

Running down the stairs to the front door, I suddenly wondered if I'd find Otto and Arturo standing on the steps, their guns drawn, but, no, there were Mom and Dad, tanned and smiling. They took turns to hug me, then came inside and climbed the stairs. They'd bought two bottles of wine for Uncle Harvey and he suggested opening them right away, but Mom and Dad both opted for tea instead.

"How's your week been?" asked Mom.

"Great," I said.

"What have you done? Come on, Tom, I want to hear everything. Where have you been? What have you seen? Tell me about your week in the big city."

I glanced at Uncle Harvey. He nodded back at me encouragingly. I tried to remember everything that we'd discussed on the plane, all the names that he had made me learn. "We went to the Metropolitan Museum," I said, ticking them off on my fingers. "The Empire State Building. The Natural History Museum. The Statue of Liberty and Ellis Island. Then we went to the Guggenheim and MoMa. Then we saw two plays, one concert, and five movies, and we went for a long walk in Central Park, and we had lunch at the Russian Tea Room, which is supposed to be one of the best restaurants in all of New York, if not the whole world."

"It all sounds amazing," said Dad. He turned to Uncle Harvey. "Thanks, bro. You've really shown him around. I hope *you've* managed to have some fun too."

"Oh, it's been great," said my uncle. "Tom is the perfect companion. We've had a really wonderful time together."

"I can see that. It's all been so cultural too. All those museums! I thought you might just spend the whole week playing computer games."

"Not once," I said, smiling proudly.

Mom was uncharacteristically silent. She was giving me one of her long, hard stares. Eventually she said, "You look different."

"What do you mean?" I said nervously. "What kind of different?"

"I don't know. Tanned, maybe. Have you been in the sun?"

"Oh, yes. The weather here's been fantastic. Probably as hot as the Bahamas."

Dad looked dubious. "I thought it had been raining all week. That's what the paper said."

"The paper must have got it wrong."

Mom was still frowning. "No, it's not just a tan. There's something about your face. You look older, somehow."

"It's only been a week," said Dad. "He can't have aged that much."

"I know he can't," said my mom. "But he has. Don't you think he looks older?"

They both stared at me. I started feeling a bit uncomfortable. I knew it was impossible, but what if they could see something in my face? What if they could see that I was lying?

"I'll tell you what it is," said my dad. "In your mind, you remember him as a little boy. You still imagine him being five years old. You haven't got used to our Tom growing up."

"He's not grown up," said Mom.

"Yes, but he's growing up. He's getting older. You'll be leaving home soon, won't you?"

"Not that soon," I said. "Give me a chance to be a teenager."

"I suppose you're right," said Mom. "You haven't changed in a week, have you?"

"No," I said.

"Maybe you just look a bit thinner. Harvey, have you been feeding him?"

"Oh, yes. All the time. I've been stuffing him like a pig."

There was a slightly awkward silence, as if no one could think of what to talk about next, and then Uncle Harvey said, "So, tea?"

Tea would be lovely, said both my parents.

"Could you give me a hand, Tom?" said Uncle Harvey.

"Sure. No problem."

I followed him into the kitchen. He put cups, milk, and sugar on a tray. "Tea for you?" he asked.

"No, thanks."

"Coffee?"

"Ha, ha."

"You never know, you might like it."

"I already know I don't."

"Fair enough." He poured boiling water into a teapot, placed it on the tray, and turned to me. In a whisper, he said, "Tom, I think you should—"

"I'm going to."

"You don't know what I was going to say."

"Yes, I do."

"Really?"

"Yes."

"How?"

"I just do."

"Go on, then. What was I going to say?"

"You were going to say you've changed your mind and you were wrong about telling lies to my parents and actually it's a really bad idea and I shouldn't do it and what I should actually do is go out there and tell them what really happened last week."

"Not bad," whispered Uncle Harvey. "Pretty good, actually. So, how about it?"

"I'm going to," I whispered back.

"When?"

"Right now." I gestured at the door. "After you."

"Oh, no. After you."

I carried some cookies into the other room and Uncle Harvey followed me with the tray. We sat down. Uncle Harvey poured the tea and I told Mom and Dad about my trip to Peru. I'd hardly started when Mom said, "If this is a joke, it's not very funny."

"Don't you want to know where I went?" I said. "Would you rather I lied to you?"

Dad told me to stop being silly, I was upsetting my mother, and they looked at Uncle Harvey as if they were appealing for help from the other adult in the room.

"The thing is . . ." said Uncle Harvey, and then he stopped. I think it was the first time I'd ever seen him lost for words. He picked up a cookie, broke it in half, and stared at the crumbs as if they held the secrets of the universe.

So I fetched my passport and showed them the stamps from Lima Airport.

Dad said, "These aren't real. They don't even *look* real. You did them yourself, didn't you?"

Before I could respond, Mom told him to keep quiet, gave me one of her looks, and said, "Is this true?"

"Yes," I said.

"Really?"

"Yes."

"You promise?"

"I promise."

Mom sighed. "You'd better tell us all about it."

So I did.

Their tea went cold. They didn't eat a single cookie. They just sat there, holding hands, listening to the story of John Drake and Otto Gonzalez and the Island of Thieves.

I expected them to be furious, but they weren't. Not at all. The opposite, actually. Before I even got to the end of the story, they both jumped up and hugged me as if they were making sure that I was really there. Then they sat down again and I told them about Miguel and Otto and the cliff and the prison and the car and coming home. Mom cried, but she said they were tears of happiness, and Dad said, "It's my fault. I'm an idiot. Why did I let him stay here? I should have known Harvey would do something like this."

Uncle Harvey was about to reply, but I jumped in first. "I told you already, he didn't want to take me with him."

"He could have—" started my dad, but I interrupted him, too.

"It's my fault," I said. "It really is. Mine and no one else's. If you want to blame anyone, blame me."

"We don't want to blame anyone," said Mom, putting her hand on Dad's knee. "You have to understand, Tom, we're still feeling quite shocked. And amazed. And not quite sure what to think. But we're not angry. Are we, Simon?"

"I am," said Dad.

"No, you're not."

"I am. I'm angry with Harvey, anyway. And I'm probably quite angry with Tom, too."

"Well, I'm not," said Mom. "I don't care what you did or where you went, or why. I'm just so glad you're safe. My beautiful boy is here. That's all I care about, Tom. Nothing else matters."

33

I *thought I wouldn't see New York again* till I was old enough to go on my own, but a month later I was back there, eating a five-course meal at the Peruvian embassy. A crisp white invitation had come in the mail from His Excellency the Ambassador. It was only addressed to me, but Mom and Dad said I couldn't go without them, so Uncle Harvey wrangled two more invites.

We had dinner in a long room lined with enormous paintings of Great Peruvians. Chandeliers hung from the ceiling and waiters carried dish after dish from the kitchens. To my relief, there was no more guinea pig, just some delicious fish and the best steak I've ever tasted. It was probably Argentinean, my uncle informed me in a whisper, not wanting to upset any proud Peruvian patriots sitting around the table.

There were ten of us. Our hosts were the ambassador and his wife. Then there was the director of the National Museum in Lima and a journalist from one of Peru's main papers, who was writing a story about us. Down at the other end of the table were the old couple from the mountains, Señor and Señora Draque.

Did you notice that name?

Yes?

You're probably wondering why we didn't.

Well, we had a good excuse. We'd never actually heard it. We couldn't speak their language and they couldn't speak ours, so we'd never introduced ourselves.

Sure, the spelling had changed a little over the years and they pronounced it in a Spanish way—kind of like "drah-kay"—but it was the same name. The same family, too. To-morrow morning, the director of the National Museum and the journalist were going to fly with the old couple to England, where they would visit Buckland Abbey, Sir Francis Drake's home. They would be staying in a hotel in Tavistock, the town where John Drake was born.

Señor Draque was going to cross the Atlantic to see the land of his ancestors. It was the first time that he had ever been out of Peru. If you'd asked him a month ago, the old man would have said he didn't have any connection to England. Now he knew he was the great-great-great-great-great-great-great-great-great-great-great-great-great-great-great grandson of John Drake.

I might have gotten the wrong number of greats, but you get the general idea. Four hundred and thirty years ago, John Drake settled in Peru and started a family. With his last breaths, he would have told his son to look after the journal that was sitting in a box under the bed. *There's a secret in there,* he would have said, *that will make you rich.*

Maybe *his* son told *his* son the same thing too. But over the years, the story had got mixed up and forgotten. No one could read the funny foreign writing on those old bits of paper. Nor was anyone quite sure why they were taking up valuable space in the house. Eventually the manuscript was yanked out to make room for some shirts or a thick wooly blanket, and dumped in the barn, scattered amongst the straw.

There it stayed until the current Señor Draque used a piece of it to wrap up an old necklace.

When we got back to New York with the manuscript, Uncle Harvey had contacted the National Museum in Lima and asked if they'd like to buy it. The director said yes. But he also said: "Where did you get it?" Uncle Harvey ummed and ahhed, but eventually admitted the truth.

Which was why Señor and Señora Draque got all the museum's money, rather than us.

Uncle Harvey was furious. The manuscript was ours, he said. After all, we had paid for it. Only sixty dollars, sure, but money is money, and the old couple had taken ours. He explained this to the director of the National Museum, who threatened to hire the most expensive lawyers on the planet and fight him in every court in the United States and Peru.

In the end, they made a deal. I don't know exactly how much the museum gave Uncle Harvey, but it was enough to pay for our flights, buy a nice shiny new car for Alejandra, and have a few dollars left over.

During the negotiations, Uncle Harvey kept quiet about the treasure. Only three people on the planet knew the actual location of the gold. Him, me, and Otto. Maybe someone in the museum would read the manuscript and work it out. If not, one day, we might go back to Peru with a team of divers and again risk the wrath of the Pacific.

At the end of the meal, we all shook hands and promised to keep in touch. Señor Draque hugged me. Señora Draque kissed me on both cheeks. The journalist took my number and said he'd call me if he had any more questions.

The ambassador escorted us to the front door. Mom and Dad walked down the stairs to the street. Uncle Harvey and I were just about to follow them when the ambassador took hold of my uncle's arm, pulling him back into the warmth of the hallway.

"I have been asked to pass on the gratitude of my government," he said, speaking in a low tone, not wishing to be overheard by my parents, the journalist, or anyone else. "We are very grateful for everything that you have done."

Uncle Harvey smiled politely. "We're just pleased the manuscript's going to have a good home in your national museum."

"I am not talking about the manuscript," said the ambassador, still speaking quietly. "I must tell you about something that happened recently in my country. There was an incident in a small village named Las Lamos. The police heard reports of shooting in a hotel. Officers were sent to investigate. They found a man lying injured in the street. He had been hit by a car. They took him to the hospital, where he was identified as a criminal named Otto Gonzalez. He is still there now, kept under armed guard while he recovers from his wounds. Then he will be taken to prison. We have wanted to capture this man for many years, but it has always proved impossible. This time we are not going to let him escape. On behalf of all our citizens, I want to thank you, Mr. Trelawney."

"You shouldn't be thanking me," said my uncle. "You should thank my nephew."

The ambassador turned to me. "I don't know what happened, Tom, and I don't want to know. But I would simply like to say, *muchas gracias.* A great threat has been lifted from our country. Thank you."

I wasn't quite sure what to say, so I just mumbled something about it not being a problem, and ended up feeling a bit stupid. The ambassador didn't seem to mind. He shook both our hands again and wished us a very good night.

The big black door swung shut and we walked down the stairs to Mom and Dad, who had been waiting in the street. That was where we said goodbye to Uncle Harvey. I'd wanted to stay the night in the city, and I think Mom wanted to too, but Dad insisted on driving home right then. "Do you want a lift?" he asked. "We could take you back to your apartment."

"Oh, don't worry," said Uncle Harvey. "I'll just take the subway." He kissed Mom on both cheeks and shook Dad's hand and then mine. "Bye, Tom," he said. "It's been a pleasure to meet you properly. You've almost made me wonder why I don't have kids of my own. If I did, I'm sure they wouldn't be half as nice as you. Or half as much fun. You will come and stay again, won't you?"

"Yes, please. When?"

"Whenever you like." He looked at Mom and Dad. "I know you probably don't trust me, but I'd look after him. I really would. And, I swear to all the gods, I'd never take him to Peru again."

"Or anywhere else?" asked Dad.

Uncle Harvey grinned. "I can't promise that. Now, I'd better go. Busy day tomorrow. Good night, Sarah. Good night, Simon." Then he turned to me. "Bye, Tom."

Before I had a chance to reply, he turned on his heel and hurried up the street toward the subway. Uncle Harvey didn't do big goodbyes. Soon he'd vanished into the crowds.

And that was that. The end of the story. Uncle Harvey went home, I drove back to Norwich with Mom and Dad, and we all lived happily ever after.

Adios!

HISTORICAL NOTE
WHO WAS JOHN DRAKE?

Francis Drake kept a book in which he entered his navigation and in which he delineated birds, trees and sea-lions. He is an adept at painting and has with him a boy, a relative of his, who is a great painter.

> — THE SWORN DEPOSITION OF NUÑO DA SILVA,
> GIVEN ON MAY 23, 1579, BEFORE THE TRIBUNAL
> OF THE INQUISITION OF MEXICO.

He is called Francisco Drac, and is a man about thirty-five years of age, low of stature, with a fair beard, and is one of the greatest mariners that sails the seas, both as a navigator and as a commander. His vessel is a galleon of nearly four hundred tons, and is a perfect sailor. She is manned with a hundred men, all of service, and of an age for warfare, and all are as practised therein as old soldiers from Italy could be . . . He also carried painters who paint for him pictures of the coast in its exact colors. This I was most grieved to see, for each thing is so naturally depicted that no one who guides himself according to these paintings can possibly go astray.

> — LETTER FROM DON FRANCISCO DE ZARATE TO DON MARTIN ENRIQUEZ, VICEROY OF NEW SPAIN, APRIL 16, 1579.

When Francis Drake sailed from England in 1577, he commanded a fleet of five ships. They left Plymouth in December and arrived in Morocco about a month later, then headed across the Atlantic to Brazil.

Drake and his crew battled hunger and thirst, storms and the Spanish. One by one, the ships sank or vanished, until a single boat was left, Drake's own, the *Pelican*, which by then had been renamed the *Golden Hind*.

Every man on the voyage had a particular job. Some cooked. Some manned the cannons. Some clambered in the rigging. And one of them kept a journal, describing what he saw, illustrating his words with drawings and maps. He was a boy, aged somewhere between ten and fourteen, and he was the cousin of the captain.

John Drake grew up in Tavistock, a little village in Devon, just north of Plymouth. His father was a farmer, and must have been rich enough to send his sons to school, because John knew how to read and write. Not many people could do either in 1577. He must have been a decent artist, too. He probably would have spent his entire life in Tavistock, working as a farmer like his dad and sketching birds and flowers in his spare time, but one day his cousin turned up and invited him on a journey to the other side of the world.

They sailed across the Atlantic, down the east side of South America and up the west, past what is now the coastline of Chile, Peru, and Ecuador. No one knows how far north they went. Definitely to Mexico, probably to California, possibly to Alaska. Then they cut across the Pacific, skirted Indonesia, touched India, stopped off in Sierra Leone, and headed back to Europe.

The voyage took three years. When the *Golden Hind* returned to England, the crew had shrunk to a third of its original size, but the ship's holds carried a vast stash of gold, silver, and spices. Drake and his sailors were rich. So were the bankers who had invested in the voyage. Queen Elizabeth didn't do badly, either: she took a fifth of all the treasure.

With his share, Francis Drake bought himself a big house in Devon. The other sailors returned to their families and settled down to enjoy their success.

John Drake wasn't even twenty, but he was already a very wealthy man. He could have spent the rest of his life frittering away his money and telling stories about his adventures. But he was too young to retire. He wanted to go to sea again. He took command of a small ship, the *Francis*, and joined another expedition to South America, searching for more gold and more adventure.

His first voyage had been a triumph, but his second seemed to be cursed. One ship disappeared in a storm. Another crew mutinied. Sailing up the River Plate, which runs between Argentina and Uruguay, the *Francis* struck a rock and sank.

John Drake waded ashore with a dozen men, carrying a few possessions. They were attacked by Indians, then captured by the Spanish. Discovering the identity of their prisoner, the Spanish marched him across the Andes to Peru. When they reached Lima, he was handed over to the Inquisition, who wanted to know everything about him and his famous cousin.

That was the last anyone heard of him. John Drake vanished. So did his journal. No one knows what happened to either of them.

He might have been killed in prison. He might have been released and allowed to board a ship heading back to Europe. Or he might have decided to stay in Peru. Perhaps he went up into the Andes, spent the night in an isolated farmhouse, and met a girl, the farmer's daughter. There he stayed, rearing goats and chickens, and started a family. On long nights in the winter, he might have pulled his journal out of a drawer and traced the spidery black handwriting with his finger, remembering old friends, distant places, a voyage around the world.

DON'T MISS THE ACTION-PACKED SEQUEL TO
ISLAND OF THIEVES:

Twelve-year-old Tom and his Uncle Harvey set off to India on another wild adventure, trying to find a jeweled tiger statue buried by one of Tom's relatives back in 1799. And as they are chased by an Australian mercenary and flee from police and man-eating tigers, Tom is finally forced to take matters into his own hands.

Turn the page for a sneak peek at *Sultan's Tigers*!

My name is Tom Trelawney and I come from a long line of liars, cheats, crooks, bandits, thieves, and smugglers.

That's what my uncle says, anyway.

I'd like to believe him, but if our family consists entirely of criminals, what went wrong with my dad? He's probably the most honest person on the planet.

"He's not a real Trelawney," says Uncle Harvey. "Not like you and me."

According to my uncle, our family originally came from a small village in Cornwall, a rugged corner of England that sticks out into the Atlantic, pointing like a finger at America. The Trelawneys called themselves fishermen, but they actually made their living by piracy, smuggling illegal goods ashore and hiding them in the caves that riddle the Cornish coast.

My grandfather was a real Trelawney too.

He wasn't a pirate or a smuggler, but he never did an honest day's work in his life. He was always running from someone, always searching for a place to hide, and he left a trail of enemies all around the world.

I never really knew him.

I wish I had.

We only saw Grandpa once a year, sometimes even less. The last time he came to the States for Christmas, he drank too much wine and had a big argument with Dad.

Ten months later, he was dead.

He had a heart attack while watching TV, and that was that, kaput, he was gone.

"A good death," my mom called it, and perhaps she's right, although it's not exactly what I'd call a good death. What's wrong with being gnawed to pieces by piranhas? Or flung from a plane without a parachute? If Grandpa had died like that, I really would have been proud of him. But he died sitting in his recliner, slumped in front of the TV, according to the neighbor who found him, so maybe that really was a good death.

Grandpa had lived all over the world, but he spent the last few years of his life in a small village on the west coast of Ireland. We arrived in Shannon at dawn on the morning of the funeral. (By "we," I mean me, my mom, my dad, my little bro, Jack, and my big sister, Grace.) Dad rented a bright blue Ford Focus at the airport and drove us across the country to Grandpa's village.

Not many people came to the funeral: just us and a few neighbors.

Halfway through the service, the door squeaked open and Uncle Harvey stumbled down the aisle. "Sorry I'm late," he whispered loudly enough for everyone to hear. The vicar gave him a stern look and carried on with the sermon. Uncle Harvey grinned at us and slid into a pew on the other side of the church. I grinned back while Dad gave him a dirty look. They might be brothers, but they don't like each other much.

I was looking forward to talking to my uncle. Earlier in the year, we had traveled to Peru together, hunting down a stash of buried gold that had belonged to Sir Francis Drake. Later, back in the U.S., we'd been given dinner at the Peruvian embassy, but I hadn't seen my uncle since. I wanted to know if he'd had any more adventures. Had he been chased by crooks? Threatened by thugs? Or beat up? Had he stolen anything? Or cheated anyone? Even after spending a week with my uncle in Peru, I didn't know very much about his life, but I knew one thing for sure: it was a lot more interesting than mine.

The ceremony concluded with prayers, then we shuffled into the graveyard and stood in line to shake hands with the vicar. When my turn came, the vicar smiled down at me and said in his warm Irish accent, "So which of the grandsons are you? Are you Jack or are you Tom?"

"I'm Tom."

"Ah, the famous Tom. Your grandfather told me all about you. He said you were full of mischief. Is that true?"

"I suppose so."

"He also said he saw himself in you. I can see what he meant."

"Really?" I said. "What else did he say?"

"Oh, this and that. Maybe I'll tell you when you're a bit older." Chuckling, the vicar let go of my hand and grabbed the next in line, which happened to belong to Uncle Harvey. "Your father was a lovely man," the vicar said. "You must be missing his presence."

"I've heard him called a lot of things," said Uncle Harvey. "But never lovely. Maybe he was lovelier to you than he was to us."

The vicar looked a bit nervous, not wanting to say the wrong thing. "I didn't know your father well, but we thought of him as a valued member of the community."

"Did you really?" Uncle Harvey sounded surprised. "So he didn't steal any of your silver? Or flog your hymn books on eBay?"

"Actually, we did have a few things go missing," said the vicar. Then he noticed that my uncle was smiling. "Ah! You're having a joke with me, aren't you?"

"I'm so sorry," said Uncle Harvey. "I can't help myself."

"Even in times of trouble, it's good to have a smile on your face." The vicar beamed and moved to talk to the next person in line.

As my uncle and I walked through the churchyard, he winked at me. I winked back. Now we knew how Grandpa had been supplementing his pension.

Uncle Harvey said, "How's life, kid?"

"It's OK. A little boring. How's yours?"

"I would say it's good, but my dad's just died so I probably shouldn't. How often did you see the old man?"

"Not very often," I replied. "He sometimes visited us for Christmas. But he and Dad always ended up arguing."

"He argued with everyone. That was just his way."

"Did you argue with him too?"

"All the time," said Uncle Harvey. "But we always made up again. He was like that. We'd get drunk together and have a big row, then forget all about it the next day. It's a pity you won't get to know him better. Did you ever come and stay with him?"

"Dad wouldn't let me. I don't know why not."

"I do," said Uncle Harvey.

"Yeah? Why?"

"He knows that as far as he's concerned, the Trelawney genes skipped a generation. You're more like your grandfather than your father. He must have been worried about what would happen if the two of you ever got together. Just like he's worried about the two of us. And he's right, isn't he? Ah, hello, Simon. How are you?"

Simon is my dad. He didn't look particularly pleased to see his brother, but maybe he was just feeling sad. I guess you would feel sad if your father died, even if the two of you had furious arguments whenever you happened to be in the same room at the same time.

The brothers shook hands. Then Uncle Harvey kissed my mom on both cheeks and said hello to Jack and Grace.

"I've invited the vicar to join us for lunch," my father said to Harvey. "Can you give him a lift in your car? There isn't much room in ours."

"Sure. Where are we going?"

"I've booked a table at a restaurant on the coast. Apparently it's very good. You can follow me there."

"Great. I'll go and get the vicar."

Once Uncle Harvey was striding across the churchyard, Dad turned to me. "Here are the keys to Grandpa's house. We'll see you there in a couple of hours."

I took the keys and stared stupidly at my father. "Why are you giving me these?"

"Because you're going to go to the house."

"What am I supposed to do there?"

"Whatever you like. Read a book, play a game. It's up to you."

"What about lunch?"

"What *about* lunch?"

"Why can't I come to lunch?"

"You know why not."

"Because I'm grounded?"

"Exactly."

"But this is Grandpa's funeral! You've got to let me come to the lunch!"

"I'm afraid not, Tom. You're grounded."

"That's so unfair!"

"You should have thought about that before you stole the golf cart. We'll be a couple of hours. See you later."

"Dad—"

"Don't 'Dad' me."

"But, Dad—"

"I said don't 'Dad' me."

"But, Dad, it's just not fair."

"See you later," said my father, showing not a trace of sympathy. "Go on. Go to the house."

Grace tried to argue on my behalf, which was nice of her, and Jack said he wouldn't mind staying with me, which was nice of him, too, but Dad asked if they both wanted to be grounded as well, and of course they didn't. He told them to go to the car. Grace grinned at me and Jack gave me a thumbs-up, then they sloped away. Dad turned back to me. "I'm sorry, Tom. I don't like doing this. I wish there were some other way. But you've really given me no choice."

I looked at my dad for a moment. Then I said, "You're an idiot."

His face turned red and he told me never to talk to him like that, and Mom said I should remember where I was, but I didn't care. I turned my back on my parents and walked away, their angry voices following me out of the graveyard.

Josh Lacey worked as a journalist, a screenwriter, and a teacher before writing his first book for children. He is the author of *Sultan's Tigers,* as well as the Misfitz Mysteries and the Grk series. Josh lives in London with his wife and daughter, and is seldom bored. Visit him online at ***www.joshlacey.com***.